SAMANTH

OFF THE
RECORD

Check out www.faithgirlz.com

faiThGirLz!™

SAMANTHA SANDERSON

OFF THE RECORD

BOOK THREE

ROBIN CAROLL MILLER

ZONDERKIDZ

Samantha Sanderson Off the Record
Copyright © 2015 by Robin Caroll Miller

This title is also available as a Zondervan ebook.
Visit www.zondervan.com/ebooks

Requests for information should be addressed to:
Zonderkidz, 3900 Sparks Drive SE, Grand Rapids, Michigan 49546

ISBN 978-0-310-74249-4

Editor: Mary Hassinger
Art direction: Deborah Washburn
Interior design: Ben Fetterley and Greg Johnson / Textbook Perfect

Printed in the United States of America

HB 09.04.2018

To Benton and Zayden...
BabyGran loves you very much!

CHAPTER ONE

L ook at you, sporting such fashion sense." Samantha "Sam" Sanderson grinned as her best friend, Makayla Ansley, joined her table in the school cafeteria before school.

Makayla nudged Sam as she dumped her backpack on the table and sat on the bench beside her. "Shut up." Makayla giggled. "You know it would hurt my mom's feelings if I didn't wear the coat they got me for Christmas."

"I know. Just teasing you." Sam scooted to make more room for her bestie on the bench. "You know I love it too. I love leather bomber jackets."

Makayla blew on the fake fur collar. "Yeah, but it's a bit much for school, don't you think?"

"Nah, girl. You're rocking it." Sam pouted her lips and snapped her fingers.

Both girls laughed.

"My, aren't you two, um, *jolly* this morning."

Sam and Makayla stopped laughing. Sam gritted her teeth and turned to face Aubrey Damas, the meanest *mean girl* in the school. She was also the school newspaper editor and constant thorn in Sam's side. Sam forced herself to remember her new year's resolution. She planted a smile and put a pleasant tone to her words. "Hi, Aubrey. Did you have a nice Christmas?"

"Of course. Daddy flew us all to Hawaii to spend the holiday on the beach." Aubrey focused on Sam. "I'll be handing out this semester's reporting assignments today in class. You don't want to be late for that, *Samantha*." She laughed — more like cackled — and moved toward a circle of her friends in the opposite corner of the cafeteria.

"She goes out of her way to be a brat," Sam muttered.

Makayla gave Sam a quick side hug. "Ignore her. She just tries to get under your skin because she's jealous of your talent."

"Hey y'all." Lana Wilson, a fellow newspaper staffer and cheerleader plopped down on the bench beside Sam and Makayla. "What'd the she-beast want?" She nodded toward Aubrey's retreating back.

Sam grinned. "To annoy me, of course." That wasn't breaking her resolution, was it?

Lana grinned back. "Same old Aubrey. So, how was your Christmas break?"

Sam twisted around on the bench, determined to

ignore Aubrey as much as humanly possible for the rest of the year. That would probably be the only way she could keep her resolution beyond this week. "Great. Mom took me on an assignment with her, which was totally cool." Going with her mother to cover a story had cemented Sam's desire to be a journalist. She had definite plans for taking the steps needed to set her on a successful career path to journalistic greatness. Outstanding reporter this year, editor-in-chief next year, then hello high school paper.

The only way Robinson High School's newspaper accepted a freshman on staff was if they'd been the editor of the middle school's paper, and getting on the high school paper staff was important. They were *very* elite in the acceptance process, and with good reason. For each of the past three years, two students from the high school had received full scholarships from the University of Missouri, which was ranked as the number one journalism college by Princeton Review. Sam planned to get a scholarship to Mizzou.

But first she had to get through this year of dealing with Aubrey and make her way to replacing her next year as editor of the Robinson Middle School's paper, *Senator Speak*. Not an easy task, that was for sure.

"That's so cool you got to see your mom work." Lana smiled.

"What about you?" Makayla asked her. "Did you have a nice holiday?"

"I did. My parents got remarried on Christmas Day."
Her eyes were bright. Her parents had been divorced
barely a year, but had been working on reconciliation.

"Oh, wow! That's awesome, Lana." Sam was truly
happy for her friend, knowing how badly Lana wanted
her parents to get back together.

"That's the best present ever," Makayla said, tears in
her eyes.

Sam shook her head. Mac could be so emotional
and wasn't afraid to show it. Sam, on the other hand,
was mortified to show emotions. Especially tears. She
refused to cry in front of anyone, period.

"I know. I'm so excited. We're going house hunting
together this weekend."

The bell rang and the cafeteria filled with noise
as everyone clamored toward their lockers. Sam led
Makayla outside through the maze of bodies to the seventh grade ramp. She shivered against the cold January
wind whipping down the breezeway. Robinson Middle
School was designed in such a way that no hallways
were enclosed. The open campus had its benefits, but
warmth during cooler weather wasn't one of them.

"Did you hear there's a chance of snow later this
week?" Makayla asked as she opened her locker.

Sam shoved her backpack in her locker and grabbed
her English book. "Yeah. I hope it does. If school's canceled, I'm sure Dad can pick you up to spend the day
with us." Her dad was a detective with the Little Rock

Police Department, but that wouldn't be why he could get Mac — he also drove a four-wheel drive truck. Sam shivered and snuggled deeper into her coat.

"Hey, we get report cards this morning don't we?" Makayla slammed her locker shut. "I hope so, because that will get Mom off my back. She nearly drove me crazy over the break, making me do practice work."

Sam laughed and hugged her books close to her chest to block some of the wind. "At least she let you start working with that computer geek group."

"It's not a computer geek group," Makayla said with a snort. "It's a computer research demographic group."

"Um, yeah. Whatever." Sam checked her watch. "Gotta run. Can't be tardy the first day back at school. See you later." And with that, she rushed off toward her homeroom for activity period.

The second bell rang just as Sam sank into her chair. She picked up the new semester schedule her teacher had placed on her desk and studied it. She would be replacing her third period keyboarding class with PE. That wasn't a big deal because she liked being active, but why couldn't they let the cheer team have a class in place of PE like the football players did? Sam sighed.

After the bell rang, signaling the end of the activity period and the beginning of first period, Mrs. Beach, the seventh grade English teacher, gave them the easiest assignment ever: write a two hundred and fifty word essay on what you did over winter break.

Sam tapped her pen against her chin. It was hard to write creatively with a pen and paper. She was much better at composing with her MacBook. There was just something about the process of having her fingers on the keyboard that made her creativity spark. Hmm. Maybe she should go at it just as if she were writing an article for the school's blog. Factual, informative, and interesting — the three rules her mom said were critical in good journalism.

"Sam," came a whisper from behind her.

She turned and smiled at Grace Brannon, also a cheerleader, seated behind her. "Hi, Grace."

"Aren't we supposed to get report cards today?"

Sam nodded. "They'll probably give them out before the end of the day."

"Last year, they gave them out with the new schedules in activity period."

Sam shrugged. "Dunno then."

"Ladies, are you ready to share your essays?" Mrs. Beach asked, staring hard at Sam and Grace.

"No, ma'am. Not quite yet." Sam turned back around in her seat while a couple of kids chuckled.

The rest of the day dragged on, as if someone had shoved peanut butter in all the school's clocks. Finally, the second bell rang for last period. Sam ran into the classroom they used for the newsroom and immediately spotted an envelope with her name sitting on her desk. She dropped her backpack on her chair and ripped open the envelope. Time for Dad to pay up. This year was going to be expensive.

Their deal was whatever grade she was in, that's the dollar amount she'd receive per A. So, if she made straight A's on her report card, she'd get forty-nine bucks because she was in the seventh grade. It was pretty cool. And if she made all A's the entire year, especially since she took advanced placement classes, Dad would surprise her with a bonus.

She hoped he planned to stop by the bank on his way home from work and get cash. He'd owe her almost fifty bucks. She pulled her report card from the envelope.

What?

Sam stared at her report card. A C in English? Seriously? On her mid-semester interim, she'd had a ninety-nine percent. Something had to be wrong. And what about that B in creative writing, the official course title for the newspaper? Had Mrs. Pape let Aubrey give input on their grades? Surely not.

Sam glanced up and realized people were raising their voices all around her. She'd been so upset about her own report card that she'd zoned out. Well, she tuned in now.

"I got an A in Science. I was almost failing on my interim."

"A D in PE? How can I get a D in PE? That's like ... it's just wrong."

"Mrs. Pape, I think you made a mistake on my report card. I know I'm not the best reporter or anything, but a C?" Luke Jensen asked.

Sam bit her tongue. Luke Jensen had sandy blond, wavy hair and eyes that reminded her of dark chocolate. In short, he was the cutest boy at Robinson Middle School. Well, to Sam anyway, not that he knew it. He barely knew that she was alive, even though they'd gone to school together since kindergarten at Chenal Elementary.

Although with the stories she'd covered for the school paper this year, he'd at least noticed her reporting abilities. That was a start, right?

"Me too, Mrs. Pape," Tam added.

Sam shook her head. No way did Tam get anything less than an A. The boy was scary smart. If he wasn't such a nice guy, Sam might actually resent his brilliance.

"I don't know what's going on. I didn't give any of you a C." Mrs. Pape sat in front of her computer monitor. "Hang on, let me check something."

In that moment of silence, Sam heard commotion from the other classrooms spilling down the hallway. Loud voices. Fear cracking in some of them.

This was more than just a couple of errors. It sounded like the entire school was on the verge of erupting into complete chaos.

"Well, do-gooder, this is a fine mess, isn't it?" Felicia Adams was the eighth grader who transferred recently after being expelled from a private school. Everyone, teachers included, thought she was bad news with an even worse attitude.

Sam saw her differently.

She learned that Felicia, who'd been a cheerleader as well as on newspaper and yearbook staff at her private school, had been forced by her mother to sit out of all extra-curricular activities at Robinson as a form of punishment. But then her mother had a change of heart and allowed Felicia to join the newspaper staff. Mrs. Trees, the principal, agreed after Felicia promised to have a 4.0 by the end of the first semester and to not get another referral to the office for a rule violation.

"My mother is going to kill me if this D in Algebra is right," Kathy Gibbs moaned, on the verge of tears. "I'll be grounded until I leave for college."

How many other kids' parents were going to go ballistic when they saw these report cards? Would they believe there was a problem with all the report cards — or at least many of them? School was set to dismiss any second now.

"I'm not sure what's going on," Mrs. Pape began.

"Teachers, boys, and girls, may I have your attention, please?" The principal's voice over the intercom silenced everyone immediately. "We understand there seems to be an issue with the report cards."

Just then, the automatic dismissal bell rang, drowning out Mrs. Trees. A chorus of kids erupted in the breezeway. Lockers slammed, swallowing the principal's announcement.

"I guess we'll learn more tomorrow." Mrs. Pape's voice was lost as the newspaper staff filed out of the classroom.

But not Sam. She reached for the wireless keyboard to one of the newspaper's computers. The report cards problem was breaking news. And maybe, just maybe, if she could get the story up on the blog, some kids might be able to show their parents there really was an issue. She ducked her head as her fingers flew over the keyboard.

"What are you doing?" Mrs. Pape stood over Sam's shoulder.

"Well ... major errors on all report cards is a big deal. It's breaking news. I thought we should get it up on our blog."

Mrs. Pape smiled. "Good thinking, Sam."

"I'm going to run up to the office and get Mrs. Trees' statement. The bell cut off her announcement."

Mrs. Pape nodded. "I'll wait for you to get back."

"Thanks." Sam grabbed her iPhone from her backpack and texted her mom as she walked.

Finishing up a story. Will be out in a few.

It was awesome that her mother was a journalist so she "got" how important following a story was. It sure made things much easier.

Sam swung open the main office door. Surprisingly, the place was packed with kids, even though the buses were already pulling out of the circle. Kids were clamoring to get the principal's attention. A couple of girls were crying.

"If you'll all just listen for a minute," Mrs. Trees started.

Sam opened the ISaidWhat?! app on her phone and pressed the record button.

"We know there's a problem with your report cards. It's too late in the day to call the district office, but I'll get in touch with them first thing in the morning to have someone look into this."

"But Mrs. Trees," one girl with tear tracks down her cheeks said, "my report card shows I got three Ds. My mother won't believe there's a problem with the report cards."

The principal nodded. "Turn your report card back in."

The girl shook her head. "My mother knows we're supposed to get our report cards today. If I don't give it to her, she'll think I'm hiding something."

Wow. Sam caught her bottom lip between her top and bottom teeth. Her mom would automatically believe her. Her dad, a detective with the Little Rock Police Department, had more of a suspicious mind, but he would believe his own daughter. Surely if this girl explained it to her mother . . .

"Hand me your report card and I'll write a note to your mother," Mrs. Trees said, holding out her hand.

The girl let out a long breath and handed her report card to the principal. "Thank you. My mother always wants proof of everything."

"Can you make a note on mine too, Mrs. Trees?"

"Yes."

"Mine too?"

"Yes, I'll write a note for everyone who needs one."

Sam stepped to the right of the forming line. "Mrs. Trees, I'm reporting on the report card errors for the school paper. The bell cut off your statement."

The principal stopped writing and glanced at Sam. "Ah, welcome back, Sam."

Sam offered a wide smile. She and the principal had an I-kind-of-like-you-but-kind-of-don't type of relationship. "What would you like to say about the mistakes?"

"We don't know what happened just yet. I'll be contacting the district as soon as I can to have someone look into the issue. Until then, I won't speculate on what the problem is." Mrs. Trees handed a report card she'd written on back to an eighth grader Sam knew to be on the football team. She took the next one from the girl standing behind him.

"Does the problem affect all the report cards?" Sam asked.

"I can't say at this time. We simply don't know." Mrs. Trees traded report cards again.

So non-committal. Sam held her iPhone closer to

the principal. "Can you tell me the process of how the report cards are run?"

Mrs. Trees handed back the last report card and gave Sam a weary look. "The system shut down this morning when we first attempted to print the report cards. Then the whole system had to be restarted. The program usually takes an hour or so to generate, then another couple of hours to print."

"Who sorts them?" Sam asked.

Mrs. Trees shook her head. "No one. We can set the system to print the report cards according to any class period. When we had to reboot the system this morning, we requested the report cards print according to seventh period. The envelope labels print in the same manner."

Interesting. Sam shifted her iPhone so the microphone faced Mrs. Trees. "Are they checked before they're put into the envelopes?" The report card envelopes were just plain brown envelopes with the district's label and the student's name printed on them.

"The names are checked. Since we had to reboot and it took the system most of the day to regenerate the report cards and then print them all for nearly fifteen hundred students, we're lucky we had time to even do that." She frowned. "Sam, that's enough. I need to get back to work." Mrs. Trees turned away from the counter and headed down the hall to her office.

Sam swiped the touch screen to close the app and dashed back to Mrs. Pape's room.

"I was wondering if you were on your way back," Mrs. Pape said as Sam burst into the classroom and headed to a computer.

Sam smiled as she accessed the paper's secure site. "Just give me a minute, and I'll get my story sent to you for proofing." She popped her knuckles and let her fingers fly over the keyboard. She didn't even need to refer to her recording with Mrs. Trees, but that was okay — she mainly wanted it for statement verification if needed. How had Aubrey let this story slip through her fingers and not jump on it herself? She should have at least assigned someone to it. Maybe she was burned out as editor.

Not Sam. When she became editor, she wouldn't be that way. She'd make sure every *possible* news item was at least followed up on, even if she had to cover everything herself.

Sam glanced at Aubrey's empty chair behind her desk. *I'll be there soon enough.*

CHAPTER TWO

So we have no idea what's going on with the report cards." Sam stabbed her last French fry with her fork and dunked it in ketchup before shoving it in her mouth. "At least the blog system was working and Mrs. Pape was able to send a post notification to all the students."

"Don't talk with your mouth full," Mom and Dad said in unison, then smiled at each other.

Eww. Icky parent affection.

Sam shuddered and swallowed. "Mrs. Pape said my article was very informative and factual. She said I just keep growing as a journalist."

Mom nodded. "I'll say. You're doing great. I'm so proud of you, my girl." She beamed. "You're a real chip off the old block." Coming from Mom, that was high praise, especially considering she was an award-winning, nationally recognized journalist.

Heat spread across Sam's face, but she didn't care. She was still riding her happy train, as Dad called her great mood. And why not? Christmas had been amazing. Mom and Dad had given her a new iMac desktop to compliment her MacBook laptop, which was beyond awesome. She'd spent the rest of her break from school playing on it and getting everything set up just so, including installing all her favorite programs.

Almost as awesome was that Makayla's parents had let her spend three nights with Sam. Three whole nights where they stayed up way too late, ate way too much popcorn, and had way too much fun together. It'd been the perfect ending to a perfect Christmas break.

"I'm proud of you too, pumpkin," Dad added. "You wrote an informative article because you wanted to help kids whose parents might not take the story at face value. Posting about there being a legitimate problem with the report cards probably kept a lot of kids out of trouble." He grinned. "Kind of like what I do at work."

Sam grinned back. "True. I guess I'm a lot like both my parents."

Mom leaned over and planted a quick kiss on Dad's cheek, then rested her head on his shoulder. "We should enjoy the moment, honey. In a couple of years, it will be like the kiss of death for her to admit she's like us in any way."

Eww. Parents kissing.

Sam grabbed her dishes and took them to the sink where she rinsed her plate and glass before putting them in the dishwasher. Thank goodness Mom was a neat freak and cleaned the kitchen while she cooked, so Sam didn't have to help clean up a mess. "I'm going to my room, okay?"

"Sure. Have lots of homework?" Mom lifted her plate and headed into the kitchen.

"Not a bunch." Sam skipped down the hall to her bedroom, her dog Chewy on her heels. She slipped inside, shutting the door behind her. Then she pulled out her cell phone and dialed Makayla's number.

"Hey, can't talk long," Makayla said quickly. "Mom's in a snit about the grades."

"How bad were the mistakes on your report card?" Sam plopped onto her bed, turned on the speaker feature, and set her iPhone on her bedside table. Chewy, her German hunt terrier, jumped up and rolled onto her back. Sam rubbed the dog's black and brown tummy.

"It shows I got two Cs. Mom about flipped. I'm glad you got an article up and the e-alert went out so I could show her."

"Yeah, I figured some kids would need something to show their parents to get them off their backs."

"Even so, Mom tried to call the school but it was either busy, or no one ever answered. What's going on?"

Sam pushed up against the headboard, pulled her MacBook onto her lap, and opened it. "I don't know. Mrs. Trees said she was calling the district office to figure it out."

"She doesn't have any idea what it could be?"

"Not a clue." Sam dug her fingers into the thick fur on Chewy's back. "It's odd, though."

"What?"

"Well, grades were changed, but as far as I know, not all of them were changed. Some grades are right. And I didn't hear of anyone getting an F."

"That is odd. It's almost like ... well, almost like the system messed up deliberately."

Sam sat upright so quickly she had to snatch her laptop to keep it from slipping off her lap. Chewy jumped off the bed, turned her medium frame around twice, then plopped onto her doggie bed beside Sam's desk. "Like grade tampering?" Sam could feel the excitement building.

"Could be, but why would somebody set the system to tamper with everyone's grades?"

"Because it would cover up a single incident."

"But what good would that do?" Sam could hear the skepticism in Makayla's voice. "You know once they get the system fixed, all the real grades will be restored."

"Maybe not." Sam adjusted her MacBook screen. "What if someone figured out a way to go into the system and change just one or two grades? They'd need a diversion to get in and change what the teacher actually entered, right?" She typed in *electronic grade tampering* into the Internet search bar and hit ENTER.

"Well, that's possible, sure. But I'm not sure it'd be worth the effort. I mean, why go through all the trouble to change so many grades and not just the one or two?" Makayla asked.

Sam pulled her scrunchie off her wrist and wrapped her long hair into a loose bun on top of her head. Her "thinking do," as Mac teasingly called it. "Maybe to avoid getting caught? I mean, after everything's ironed out and supposedly fixed, if one or two grades are still found to be incorrect, the student can always claim they know nothing and no one would question that, right?"

"Hmm. You have a point. So you think this isn't a glitch in the system but a deliberate act connected to grade tampering?"

"You sound a lot like my dad when you talk that way, Mac." She clicked on one of the result links from the Internet search. "Listen to this story about a Florida college case," she read. "Two students allegedly used a keylogger to monitor when instructors used their passwords and usernames to log into the school's computer system. The students allegedly used that information to access the grading systems and change grades, according to officials. One of the students reportedly changed his grades in over a dozen different classes and the grades of more than fifty students dating back a couple of years. Most students, however, were not aware their grades were changed, according to police."

"Wow."

Sam nodded, even though her best friend couldn't see her. "See, even in this instance, they changed a lot of other grades so the changing of one or two of theirs wasn't so obvious. It makes it harder to prove who's responsible."

"I would never have thought of that."

Of course she wouldn't. Makayla was one of the most honest and good people Sam knew.

"How did they get caught?" Makayla asked.

"When a teacher noticed the grades entered in the grading system didn't match what she had on her gradebook. Apparently, she's one of the few professors who still keeps an actual written gradebook." Sam went to the next result link.

"That's crazy."

"Here's another one. This one is at a high school in California." Sam summarized the news article: "Three high school juniors supposedly broke into classrooms, hacked into four teachers' computers, and changed their grades online. The teachers were unaware their computers had been hacked and grades changed until a student brought the information to the attention of the principal and teachers noticed discrepancies in their bookkeeping."

"I don't even know what to say," Makayla said.

"Listen to this." Sam read aloud, "The principal said the culprits were very bright kids — in advanced placement and honors classes."

"Sam, do you really think that's what's happened here?"

"I don't know, Mac, but you have to admit, it's a real possibility. We can't deny the facts of these other cases. And there are more than just those two." Sam scrolled through the long list of search results. "Many more."

"Oops, I've gotta go, Sam. Mom's hollering for me. See you in the morning."

Sam cleared her cell, but kept staring at the laptop monitor. Everything Mrs. Trees had told her about the incident pointed straight to grade tampering. It was what made the most sense.

But who?

Sam popped her knuckles and opened up a new blog post template. She needed to be ahead of the news to make sure she stayed assigned to this story. Aubrey already had to be livid about her earlier post today, as was typical Aubrey fashion whenever Sam did anything that distracted from Aubrey herself. The she-beast would be out for blood tomorrow, and looking for any reason to give the story to someone — anyone — else.

Sam quickly typed up a blog post, the words stringing together much, much faster than her essay in

English had today. She finished and read it over. Good, but Sam still wasn't satisfied. It was a lot of the same information she'd already posted that she'd gotten from Mrs. Trees. Just a replay of the facts.

A thought occurred to her. Was the eschoolplus system messed up as well? She typed in the URL and hit enter.

Eschoolplus was the web-based program the school utilized. School and district administrators, teachers, parents, and even students used the program to easily access and manage student information — like attendance records, grades, homework assignments, and even discipline issues. Everything was there.

Once the site loaded on her laptop, Sam logged on and went to the report cards page, and searched for the current reporting period's cards. Sure enough, the grades listed there were the same ones printed on her report card. The corruption was in the entire system. Sam stared at the screen. Was the whole software system jeopardized, just the district's, or just the school's?

She checked the school district's webpage and nearly catapulted off her bed. They had her article up on the site. And *ohmygummybears* ... With. Her. Byline!

Hopping off her bed, she did her happy dance. Chewy jumped up and ran in circles around her feet, excited just because Sam was.

Calm it, girl. Sam took in a slow breath, then let it out even slower. She sat back down on the bed and pulled the MacBook back on her lap. She scrolled down the school district's page. There was no other article or posting about report card errors at any other school in the district. Hmm. Did that mean the problem was isolated to Robinson?

Sam ran an Internet search to see if there were any posts regarding report card errors today. There were a lot of Twitter and Facebook posts about the issue, but all from kids at her school. Even a couple of Instagram pictures of report cards, but nothing outside of her school. She also checked a couple of her Facebook friends who went to Robinson High, but there was no mention of a problem with their report cards.

So the incident must be isolated to Robinson Middle School.

Sam typed quickly as she edited her article to include this new information. Once she did a final read-over, she attached it to an email and sent it to Mrs. Pape to upload to the school blog's servers. At the last second, she decided to copy Aubrey on the email as a courtesy.

Aubrey would flip her lid, but what else was new? Aubrey always went out of her way to cause problems for Sam. This time would be no different. Sam figured Mrs. Pape would tell her tomorrow that she should've waited for approval from Aubrey before emailing it to her to upload, but Sam knew Aubrey would figure out a way to take the story from her. At least she'd get two posts in before Aubrey snatched it away.

One had already gotten her up on the district's website. That alone was worth the drama she'd have to deal with tomorrow.

CHAPTER THREE

... Sound Off, Senators, and leave a comment as to what YOU think happened with the report card fiasco — grade tampering or computer glitch. ~ Sam Sanderson reporting.

"Samantha Sanderson!"

Sam gritted her teeth, rolled her eyes at Makayla, then rose from the cafeteria bench to face Aubrey Damas. "Yes, Aubrey?" She really wasn't up to such drama before school even started.

"How dare you take it upon yourself to cover a story and post not one, but two articles without authorization!" If smoke could really come out of someone's ears, Aubrey would be setting off every smoke alarm within a five-mile radius.

"Actually, Aubrey, isn't it obvious that Mrs. Pape approved the article yesterday? That's kind of how the e-alert went out." Only Mrs. Pape and school and district officials could activate the email and text alert system. Sam flashed Aubrey a snarky smile. "Mrs. Pape was pleased that someone on the paper's staff cared enough about such an important story to put in the extra time to interview Mrs. Trees and get the story out." She kept smiling and lifted a shoulder in a casual shrug. "And the district must have thought it worthy since they put it up on their page last night."

Aubrey's blue eyes squinted until they looked like nothing more than teensy tiny slits under her eyebrows. Her face turned a dark red, and her hands curled into fists at her sides.

Sam took a step backward, just in case Aubrey exploded. No sense getting Aubrey-ick all over herself.

"There are already over four hundred comments on your post, Sam." Lana Wilson plopped down at the cafeteria table beside Makayla and grinned up at Sam and Aubrey. "A lot of parents are even chiming in. Isn't that awesome, Aubrey?" Lana widened her smile.

Sam pressed her lips together to stop the laughter from spilling out. Lana knew how much Aubrey hated when Sam got positive attention, and she liked to rub salt in Aubrey's wounds every chance she got. This time, it was like she'd poured a whole shaker full.

Makayla nodded. "What wonderful exposure for

the *Senator Speak*. And, Aubrey, everyone must be impressed with your leadership as editor." Makayla, ever the peacemaker, smiled sweetly and genuinely.

Sometimes, just sometimes, Sam wished Mac wasn't such a nice person. It was nice to see Aubrey squirm occasionally. It didn't make up for all the times she went out of her way to be mean, but it was nice when the tables were turned and everything didn't go the way she wanted.

That wasn't a very nice sentiment for a Christian, Sam realized. During last Sunday's youth meeting, Ms. Martha, the youth leader, had encouraged the group to find a Scripture and to base one of their new year's resolutions on. Sam had chosen Matthew 22:39: *Love your neighbor as yourself*, because it made her immediately think of Mrs. Willis, their next door neighbor. Mrs. Willis was a widow who lived alone and was always willing to pick Sam up from school if her parents were busy. Sam had chosen the resolution so that she'd be more aware of Mrs. Willis being alone and needing a friend.

Once she took on the Scripture as her resolution, Sam realized it wasn't just about her physical neighbor, but also neighbors in the whole community. And that included Aubrey.

Which would push and try Sam all year.

Aubrey still looked ready to spit nails, but Makayla had managed to diffuse her from blowing up. "Be that as it may, *Samantha*, we need to go see Mrs. Pape." Aubrey straightened her shoulders. "Now."

Sam grabbed her backpack and slung it over her shoulder. "Catch you later, Mac."

Makayla threw her a "be nice" look. "See you."

Aubrey led the way from the cafeteria toward the eighth grade ramp where Mrs. Pape's classroom was. "Don't think I don't know what you're up to, Samantha Sanderson."

"What?" Sam feigned innocence as she pulled her coat tighter around herself. A fierce wind whipped down the breezeway.

"You're trying to show me up, but you won't do it. I'm on to you." Aubrey's eyes were narrowed and her hands were fisted onto her bony hips.

"Aubrey, I'm just trying to be the best reporter I can be." That was the truth.

"Yeah. Sure. Right. You think just because your mom is a hotshot reporter, you're all that. Well, I'm here to tell you that doesn't matter."

Sam stopped and stared at Aubrey. "Is that what you think? I don't think that at all. I want to be as good as my mom so I try to be the best reporter. That's all."

Aubrey snorted and opened Mrs. Pape's door. "Whatever. But you just remember this, Samantha Sanderson, I'm the editor here." She turned and faced their teacher sponsor. "I found Samantha, Mrs. Pape." She smiled sweetly as she set her backpack on the desk.

It was like she shrugged off her mean girl persona as simply as she shucked off her coat.

Talk about split personality city.

Mrs. Pape sat on the edge of her desk. "Hi, Sam. Your article's getting a lot of attention this morning."

"Yes, ma'am." She braced herself for the lecture to come.

"I'm sure you researched the facts?"

Sam nodded. "I have links to a couple of the news reports I referenced about high school grade tampering."

"Good." Mrs. Pape glanced at Aubrey, then back at Sam. "District sent an IT team here early this morning."

This wasn't a lecture at all ... she was giving Sam information. Sam curbed her excitement and pulled out her iPhone. She opened the Notes app and began typing. "Have they found anything yet?"

"As far as they can tell, a grade tampering virus is to blame, and it's only embedded in the grading program, not the whole computer system. That's why we're still able to use the other programs on the system."

"A virus?" She hadn't really thought about that, but now that it was out there, that's the only thing that made sense. She remembered enough from talking with Makayla to know that whoever did this had to use a virus for all the code to worm its way into the system and make the random changes it did.

"According to the team, the virus has only affected our school, and only the grading program."

Sam thought about that as she typed. "But, Mrs. Pape ... the grades are affected in eschoolplus, which is a web-based district program. We use the district's network to send our school's information."

"Correct. The IT team reported that the virus was infiltrated on one of the computers in our school and since we only send data related to our school grades to the website, the virus didn't spread to the rest of the district's eschoolplus information, or to any other program on our system."

Sam nodded, even as her fingers flew over the touchscreen. "So the IT team is sure the virus started here at school?"

Mrs. Pape nodded. "They're positive."

This was bigger than she'd originally thought. Someone had to be pretty good to build a virus like this. Sam stared at Mrs. Pape. "I'm assuming since you called me in that I'll get to stay on the story?" She snuck a glance at Aubrey. Maybe she'd had a chance to cool off and wouldn't snatch the story away from her.

"Aubrey?" Mrs. Pape prompted.

Aubrey sighed and rolled her eyes. "Yes, you get to stay on the story. But only because your dad has been assigned to the case."

So that's why she'd keep the assignment. Not because she'd been doing a great job, but because they wanted her to use her relationship with her dad to get information. It hurt her feelings a little. She should be used to it by now, but it still stung.

Mrs. Pape continued, unaware of Sam's feelings. "The staff are all a bit on edge because most of us utilize the computer system solely for our grading purposes. If the grades can't be restored, we'll have to try and work manually, which isn't ideal. Some teachers aren't even sure they could."

Interesting. Sam chewed her bottom lip. "Dad's been assigned to the case? As in, this is a police matter?"

Mrs. Pape nodded. "Oh, this could be very serious. Charges can be misdemeanor and felony."

"As soon as Mrs. Trees learned it was a virus and only affected this school, she called the police," Aubrey said.

"They just called back and told Mrs. Trees that your dad and his partner would be here soon," Mrs. Pape added.

"Oh. Okay." Sam's mind raced. Had Mrs. Pape pushed Aubrey to let Sam stay on the story just because she knew Dad was on the case and on his way?

The bell rang for kids to go to their lockers.

Sam grabbed her backpack.

"We can discuss future articles in class," Mrs. Pape said.

Sam nodded, but kept heading toward her locker. She didn't want Aubrey to see the defeat that was surely written all over her face.

"Hey, what's wrong?" Makayla asked as soon as Sam joined her at their lockers.

Yep, something sure showed in her expression. Or maybe it was just that Mac knew her so well.

"Sam?"

She quickly filled her bestie in on what Mrs. Pape and Aubrey had said.

"I'm so sorry, Sam." Makayla gave her a quick hug. "But that doesn't mean you aren't a great reporter. Remember, you cared enough to write that first article before your dad was called in."

"Yeah." That didn't make her feel much better.

"And the district thought it was so awesome that they put it on their page."

That made her feel a little better. "I guess."

"Shake it off, girl. Just be your usual good self. Everybody knows you're the best reporter on staff."

Sam smiled. Mac always cheered her up. She gave her bestie a side hug and slammed her locker. "Thanks, Mac."

Mac smiled. "See you at lunch."

Sam made fast tracks to English class and barely slipped into Mrs. Beach's classroom before the second bell sounded.

Mrs. Beach took attendance, then passed out the worksheets for classwork.

"Hey, did you hear about Luke Jensen?" Grace whispered once Mrs. Beach had returned to her desk.

Sam's heart hiccupped and she twisted in her chair. "What about him?"

"He was sent to the office because Mr. Emmitt thought he might have had something to do with the grade tampering thing."

"What? Luke Jensen?" She shook her head. "No way."

Grace shrugged. "I'm just telling you what I heard."

Sam turned back in her chair and stared at the worksheet, but she couldn't read anything. Luke Jensen? She'd gone to school with him since kindergarten. He wasn't in AP classes and he didn't make straight A's. He had mostly all B's, but that was hardly a reason to need to change his grades. She turned back to Grace. "Why would Mr. Emmitt think Luke had something to do with the grade tampering?"

Grace shrugged again. "Dunno. Just what I heard."

Sam stared at the board but didn't really see it. Someone had to have heard wrong. Luke Jensen couldn't be involved. He just couldn't.

CHAPTER FOUR

I need to talk to you."

Sam looked up from her almost-finished lunch to meet Felicia's stare. "Okay. Sit down." She waved at the space beside her on the cafeteria bench.

Felicia shook her head. "I need to talk to you alone." She tossed Makayla a weak smile. "No offense."

Mac smiled brightly. "None taken."

"Well, I'm about done anyway." Sam stood and grabbed her tray and coat. "See you outside in a few minutes?" she asked Makayla.

"Sure."

Sam threw away her trash, slipped on her coat, then followed Felicia outside to the recess area. They sat on one of the empty spaces on the benches. "So, what's up?" Sam asked once they were settled.

"About your article. Where did you come up with the idea of grade tampering?"

"Mac and I were talking on the phone and it just came up. I did some Internet research and the idea seemed possible. Why?"

Felicia looked around, then leaned closer to Sam and lowered her voice. "You know I was expelled from my previous school, right?"

Sam nodded.

"Do you know what I was expelled for?"

Sam grinned. "For being a troublemaker?" It was the nickname Sam had bestowed upon Felicia, in a friendly way, of course.

But Felicia didn't smile. She shook her head. "I was expelled for suspected grade tampering."

The smile slipped off Sam's face. "What?"

"It's not like this, and it's not as bad as it sounds."

Grade tampering, no matter how you looked at it, was bad. Period.

"Just listen. Give me a chance to explain." Felicia's bad girl demeanor had disappeared.

Sam nodded slowly. "Okay."

Felicia let out a long breath. "Our eighth grade Algebra teacher was the hardest. Even harder than the advanced placement Algebra class here. She's flunked more kids than any other teacher at the whole school."

Sam crossed her arms, as much as a defensive move as to keep warm.

"Anyway, my best friend was in her class with me. Angie is a sweetheart. You'd really like her. She's always helping someone and doing something nice for people."

Sam didn't comment.

"Anyway," Felicia continued, "Angie has wanted to be a model for forever, and finally talked her mom into letting her submit a portfolio and application. That was back in the summer. She hadn't heard back from them and had tried to put it out of her mind. Finally, right after Thanksgiving, the agency contacted her. She was given a date and time to audition for the agency. The only problem was, it was during school hours. She begged her mom and finally, her mom agreed to let her miss school that afternoon to go to the audition."

Well, that made sense. Sam's mom, and even her dad, would let her miss school for something really important she wanted to do.

"The day before the audition, our Algebra teacher announced she'd be giving a nine-week test the next day. If we failed the test, we'd fail the class. Angie asked if the test could be made up. Our teacher said no, but if anyone was planning on missing the *next* day, they could take it *that* day."

"Without studying or preparing?"

"I know. It was crazy." Felicia shook her head. "But Angie didn't have a choice. She couldn't tell her mom and miss the audition, and she couldn't get a zero in Algebra. So she went ahead and took the test."

A group of boys came by, tossing a basketball. "Hey, Sam ... I saw your dad this morning. Are the cops involved in the report card problem?" one of them asked.

"You'll have to wait and read my next article to find out," she told him.

Once the boys moved on, Felicia continued. "After school, Angie bawled. She told me she'd taken the test and knew she'd failed it. If she flunked Algebra, her mom would never let her do any modeling, even if she was accepted at the agency. She didn't know what to do." Felicia stared out across the recess area.

Makayla and Lana crossed the yard. Makayla gave a little wave to Sam.

And Sam understood. "You changed Angie's test grade?"

"No."

Sam wrinkled her nose.

Felicia smiled. "I went into my cheerleading coach's computer, accessed the school's database, and got into the Algebra teacher's gradebook. Yes, I intended to change Angie's failing grade to a passing one."

"But you couldn't do it at the last minute?" Sam asked.

"You think better of me, do-gooder. No, I didn't change her grade at all. Turns out it didn't need changing. She'd scored an eighty-eight on the test. Passed with flying colors."

"So you didn't tamper with any grades?"

"I didn't, but the thing is, our private school had an alert on its computer systems. As a security measure, if a teacher accessed another teacher's records, an alert was sent to both teachers and the principal."

"Oh."

Felicia nodded. "Yeah. It wasn't hard to figure out that I was the one who accessed my coach's computer and got into my Algebra teacher's records."

"So they knew you could have changed Angie's records?"

"No, they thought I was trying to change some of mine. You see, I had a very, very low grade in that class. If I made less than eighty-nine on the nine weeks test, I would have flunked Algebra for the nine weeks. They thought I was upping some of my classwork grades to offset a bad test score."

"They didn't believe you when you told them the truth?"

Felicia shook her head. "I didn't tell them. I didn't want them to make Angie re-take the test and there be a chance she not score as well on it. It would've been just like our teacher to give Angie a much harder replacement test."

"So what did you do? Say you did something you didn't?" Sam would, of course, take blame if it meant protecting Mac, even though she probably wouldn't let Sam do it. "Didn't Angie come forward with the truth?"

"Angie didn't know what I had done. She had no idea. Still doesn't."

Sam swallowed the lump in her throat. What Felicia meant to do was wrong, but protecting her friend ... well, Sam had to admire that. "So what did you say?"

Felicia shrugged. "I admitted to using Coach's computer and going into my Algebra teacher's records. I said I looked at grades, but didn't change a single thing."

"They didn't believe you?"

Felicia snorted. "Seriously? Of course not, but it didn't matter. Because I'd accessed unauthorized information, I'd broken school rules. The punishment for the violation was expulsion." Felicia sat back and hugged her coat around her. "So there you have the whole story."

"Wow, Felicia. I'm not sure what to say." Sam couldn't say she wouldn't do the same for Mac.

"The problem is, since you brought up the possibility of grade tampering, Mrs. Trees has been keeping an eye on me. Especially since our deal is if I have less than a four-point-oh, I'm kicked off the newspaper staff. They've called my mother to come up for a meeting after school. Apparently the police will be here too." Felicia looked around and lowered her voice again. "I'm just starting to like this place and now ... well, I'm scared of what Mom might do."

Sam chewed her bottom lip. She believed Felicia and didn't want to hurt her feelings or make her angry, but she had to ask the question. "You had nothing to do with this, right?"

The hurt marched across Felicia's face. She jumped to her feet. "I thought you were different. I thought I could trust you. Guess I was wrong." She turned to stomp off.

Sam grabbed her arm. "Felicia, I had to ask. You know you would too."

Felicia glared at her.

Sam's heart pounded. "Come on. You know I believe you. If you tell me you had nothing to do with this, I believe you. I just have to know the truth."

"I had nothing to do with this. Any of it," Felicia spat out.

"I'm sorry I had to ask, but you'd do the same." Sam tugged on the sleeve of her coat. "Sit down. Please."

Felicia hesitated for a minute, then sat back down.

"Look, you didn't do anything wrong, so there's no reason to be scared."

"Didn't you hear me, Sam? I was expelled from a school barely nine weeks ago for grade tampering. Now, here at this school, there's a serious incident of grade tampering." Felicia shook her head and let out a long breath. "You really think they're not going to think I'm involved? Wake up, do-gooder, and get real."

"First off, of course they're going to talk to you. They'd be stupid not to, and stop looking at me like that. They're only doing what they should and you know it." Sam tapped her chin and stared off at the football field across the lot. "But you did nothing wrong, so you know there's no proof against you."

"But my expulsion ... Sam, I admitted going into the system unauthorized. Do you really think they're going to require proof?"

"This isn't a private school. They have to have proof. They can't just suspend or expel you without it."

Felicia shook her head. "But they've called in the police."

"Yep. My dad and his partner." Wait a minute ... was that why Felicia had sought her out to tell her everything? Because she knew Sam's dad was heading up the case? Was everybody going to use Sam because of her father?

"Your dad is on the case?" Felicia sounded surprised.

Maybe she didn't know and she really came to Sam for advice. "So I hear, although I haven't talked to Dad since before school."

"But if he is, you can explain it to him?"

If Sam could help a friend, she would. Talk about loving her neighbor. "No, but you can. Dad and Detective Roscoe, his partner, both will listen to the truth."

"I'm scared. My mom will just react, especially with the police being there."

"Nothing to be scared of. Dad will hear you out, just like I did."

"Will ... Will you come with me? To the meeting, I mean?"

Sam shook her head. Sure, she wanted the story, but she didn't want to get in the middle of something like this. Dad would not be pleased. He wouldn't appreciate her butting in.

Felicia spoke faster. "Please? I'll do all the talking. It'll just make me feel better having you there. And it'll show my mom that I'm not just a trouble-maker, but that I'm trying. I mean, I'm making friends here and everything and I'm making good grades, but she might think I'm not and I'm trying to change them and — "

"What do you know about creating a computer virus?" Sam interrupted.

Felicia frowned. "A computer virus? Nothing. Why? What's that got to do with anything?"

"Are you good with computers? Writing HTML code? Running systems? Any type of programming?" Sam pushed. She, herself, wasn't as good as Makayla, but she knew enough to ask the right questions.

"Not really. Why?"

"No reason." She patted Felicia's arm. "You're going to be fine."

"Sam, I don't understand."

The bell rang, signaling the end of second lunch period.

"Just tell the truth and you'll be fine." Sam stood.

"Please go to the meeting with me, Sam. I'm begging you."

Sam stared into Felicia's face. Her eyes. Every little bit of her expression screamed her fear.

"Pretty please? It'd mean the world to me, do-gooder."

How was saying no being loving to her neighbor? "Okay. I'll go with you as a show of support."

"Thank you." Felicia gave her a hug, but she broke away faster than fast, glancing around. "Okay, I'll see you in last period." She turned and rushed off.

"What was that all about?" Makayla asked, coming up to link her arm through Sam's as they headed to their lockers.

"A big ole mess." She quickly told Makayla about her talk with Felicia because, hey, Felicia hadn't said she couldn't say anything, right?

"Wow. Wish I could be there for that meeting." Makayla shut her locker.

"Maybe you can. I'm sure Dad would drive you home."

Makayla shook her head. "Can't. It's Tuesday. Karate practice, remember?"

Getting back into the regular routine after the holidays was tough. Sam nodded. "Call me when you get home." She turned and ran toward her class.

As Sam took her seat and pulled out her notebook, she had a hard time concentrating. She needed to figure out who was behind the grade tampering and fast, before Felicia took the blame for it. Everyone was looking for the person responsible, and the principal and district would want the situation resolved soon. With Felicia's past, it'd be easy to pin the blame on her and let her take the fall.

Way too easy.

CHAPTER FIVE

I t's going to be fine. Remember that. Just tell the truth," Sam told Felicia as they made their way to the office after school.

The heat hit them as they entered the office, right at the entrance of the school.

Mrs. Darrington, the school secretary, looked up as they entered. "Oh. Felicia. Mrs. Trees is waiting for your mother to arrive." She glanced at Sam and narrowed her eyes. "Are you supposed to be here?"

"Is my dad here yet?" Sam evaded the question.

"He'll be here soon. I didn't realize you were going to be in their meeting. You girls go ahead and have a seat on the bench outside Mrs. Trees' office."

"She really despises me," Felicia whispered as they

huddled down the hall to the bench. "I don't think she has a good side."

Sam silently agreed. Her palms were a little sweaty, and it didn't have anything to do with the smothering heat blowing in the office. What was Dad going to say when he saw her? He'd be upset, to say the least. He'd tell her all about how she shouldn't get into everybody else's business. This time was different, though. Felicia had begged her to come. She licked her lips, trying to think of what she would tell him.

They rounded the corner of the hallway by the principal's office, and Sam stopped suddenly. Her heart skipped a beat.

"Hey, Sam. What're you doing here?" Luke Jensen asked, flashing her an almost automatic smile before he grimaced, as if remembering where they were.

Sam's mouth wouldn't form any words. There was something about Luke ... he had the deepest dimples that should have to be registered because they were so deadly cute.

A minute passed with Sam just standing and staring. Then another.

Felicia dropped onto the bench and pulled Sam down to sit next to Luke. "She's here for moral support for me." She tossed Sam a look that clearly asked are-you-stupid-or-what? "What are you doing here?" Felicia asked Luke.

Luke's face turned red.

"Mrs. Trees called me in. And she called my dad. He'll be here any minute, and I bet he won't be happy."

"Why?" Sam choked out, still a little tongue-tied.

"Mr. Emmitt told Mrs. Trees I might have had something to do with the report cards being messed up." Luke's annoyance was plain on his face.

"Why would he say that?" Felicia asked.

"We had to turn in our science project plan a few weeks ago, right?"

Sam nodded.

"Well, mine is based on the creation of a numeric-altering computer algorithm." He leaned back against the bench, stretching his long legs out into the hallway.

To Sam, he still looked annoyed. Maybe he was worried that his dad and Mrs. Trees would blame him without hearing him out. That would make her concerned, for sure.

"I'm sorry, I'm not following how that has anything to do with the grades getting changed," Felicia said, her brows bunching together.

"Apparently such an algorithm, or one like it, could be used to create major problems in a grading system. Like what's happened with our report card problem."

Sam's reporter instincts overrode the frustrating effects of Luke, and she morphed into total investigation mode. "Is that what you intended? With your project, I mean?"

He shook his head. "Not even close."

"Then what was your science project all about?"

"Well — "

"Sam, what are you doing here?"

She stood and smiled, wiping her palms on her jeans. "Hi, Dad. Hi, Detective Roscoe."

"Hey, Sam. How goes it?" Detective Roscoe asked, his smile bright against his smooth, dark skin.

"Again, Sam, what are you doing here?" Dad asked in his "detective dad" voice.

"Felicia." A woman, probably a little older than Sam's mom, joined them. "What's going on?"

"Hi, Mom." Felicia's voice was weaker than Sam had ever heard it, and she looked downright terrified.

Mrs. Trees opened her office door. "Mrs. Adams?" Felicia's mom nodded.

"Come in and have a seat." Mrs. Trees stepped aside to let Felicia's mother enter. "Felicia." She turned to Sam's dad. "Detectives Sanderson and Roscoe." She waved them inside.

Sam didn't know what to do, but Felicia circled back to grab Sam's arm and pull her into the office with them. Felicia took a seat beside her mother, wearing a look of pure panic. Dad leaned against the wall, his eyebrows raised. For a moment, Sam faltered. Annoying Dad was never a good option. But she'd told Felicia she'd be there, and in light of her resolution to love her neighbor, she didn't really feel guilty. A gray-haired man wearing a dark suit and blue tie — a man Sam had never seen before — sat beside Mrs. Trees' desk, which was covered with papers, pink phone messages, and one of those cool USB drives that look like a real key. This one had a picture of a zebra head on it.

"Samantha, you aren't needed," Mrs. Trees said, frowning.

"I asked her to come, Mrs. Trees," Felicia offered, her voice barely over a whisper.

"I don't think you understand, Felicia," Mrs. Trees began. "This isn't a discussion you can feel free to invite people to attend. This is my meeting, and I decide who will be present." She looked over at Sam. "Go out in the waiting room and shut the door behind you." She glanced at Sam's dad, then looked at Sam again. "Please."

Felicia's face went white.

Sam took a deep breath and looked at her father.

"Have a seat outside, Sam." His tone was light, but she recognized it well. He wouldn't tolerate further discussion. *So much for not feeling guilty, but they just don't understand.*

She mouthed, "I'm sorry" to Felicia, and stepped back into the hall, shutting the door behind her.

"What's going on?" Luke asked.

Sam sat back on the bench beside him and let out a long breath. "Mrs. Trees called Felicia and her mom to a meeting just like she did with you and your dad."

"So I'm not the only one they think might have had

something to do with the grade changes?" Hope made him look even cuter, if that was possible.

If he was hopeful that someone else was responsible, didn't that mean beyond a doubt that he wasn't involved? Surely he wouldn't be happy someone else would get blamed?

She cleared her throat and stared at the closed office door. "Apparently there are at least a couple of suspects."

"Your dad's the cop investigating it?"

She let out another long breath. "So it seems."

An awkward silence followed. Sam wanted to ask him questions about his science fair project, but whenever she looked at him, it was as if she was either mute or incapable of forming complete sentences.

"Can I tell you something?" he asked.

She looked up quickly and nodded.

"You can't tell anyone. I mean, not even your dad."

Sam looked into his eyes and nodded again. It didn't matter what he said, his eyes were mesmerizing. They were big and —

"I don't even know what the science project is about. Seriously."

"W-What?" Sam gave her head a little shake. Maybe she'd misunderstood him.

"It wasn't even my idea. My older brother helped me with the project so I could bring my C up to a B and my dad would stop threatening to pull me out of sports."

Sam tried to force her brain to focus on his words, but she still didn't understand. "I'm not following you."

"My dad is always harping on me to keep at least a three-point-oh average. He says that if I drop below that, he'll pull me out of all my sports."

"I get that. My dad always says that if my grades fall, I will have to give up extracurricular stuff to concentrate on my studies."

"Man, do parents get some sort of manual that tells them this stuff?"

Sam grinned. "Probably."

"Anyway, my brother goes to Mills High School and helped me with it because he's tired of hearing dad harp on me all the time. Besides, he says I'm a good defensive lineman and Robinson High's football team needs me."

That was a year and a half away, so Sam moved on. "So what does the project do?"

"That's what I'm saying ... I don't even really know."

"What? How can you not know what your project does?"

"Mark's in the scholar program at Mills and he's into computer programming and all that. Part of the project was based on being able to take figures and averages of sporting numbers and run a program that would figure probabilities and possibilities."

Sam shook her head. "So what does that have to do with changing grades?"

"It doesn't, but Mr. Emmitt says that the coding I proposed *could* be used to get into a system like a grading system and change percentages of grades."

"That's crazy to even think that."

"Yeah, I think so too, but he told Mrs. Trees that he was suspicious of me because my project plan was, get this, *a bit above Luke's usual level of work*. Can you believe that? I mean, is he calling me stupid, but in a polite way or what?"

Harsh.

Luke shook his head, looking disgusted. "And the worst part is I can't even really explain it since Mark was the one who actually did the work. I mean, he quickly showed me how, but I don't remember any of that stuff. It doesn't stick so well for me." He gave a small smile but returned to his thoughts. "I can't tell them that, though. Not with my dad there. He'll really yank me out of sports and probably the paper too."

Sam leaned toward him, struggling to keep her voice low even though she was excited. "You have to tell them, Luke. Otherwise you're a suspect."

"I can't. My dad will totally freak. And it wouldn't just be me. It'd get Mark in hot water with Dad too."

Man, this was truly a tough one. "There has to be some way."

"As soon as I go in there and they start asking me about the project, they're going to realize real fast that I don't know what I'm talking about."

"Maybe they'll realize how absurd it is that they think you're the culprit."

Luke shook his head again. "They'll probably think I'm hiding something and really blame me." He ran his hands through his hair. "There's no way out of this one."

A thought occurred to Sam. "Did Mark realize the program he helped you propose could be used like this? I mean, after he heard about the report cards?"

"Nope. He laughed it off last night when we talked about it at dinner, even saying he was glad his school didn't have any problems since he made straight As on his report card and didn't want that messed up."

"Is the program done? Finished, I mean?"

Luke grunted. "The preliminary part has already been turned in, but the actual project isn't finished just yet. Mark's been studying for his semester exams."

"Luke?" a big, burly man lumbered down the hallway.

"Hi, Dad." Luke's tone was apprehensive.

Sam could see why. Luke's dad had to be over six feet tall, and his shoulders were as wide as an Arkansas Razorback's front lineman. He was intimidating, to say the least.

"What's going on, son?" Luke's dad tossed a quizzical look at Sam before focusing on Luke.

"I'm not real sure. It has something to do with our report cards being messed up, but — "

"Luke, what did you do?" Mr. Jensen's voice sounded like a growl.

"Nothing, Dad. I promise I didn't do anything."

"Then why are we here? Principals don't call parents to come in and discuss an issue if it isn't serious." He stared at Sam again.

She fought the urge to squirm under his scrutiny. She certainly hadn't done anything wrong.

The door to Mrs. Trees' office swung open. Felicia and her mother stepped outside. Felicia's face was splotchy. Her eyes were puffy and red. Sam stood, but Felicia gave a little shake of her head. Without a word, she followed her mother down the hall and out of sight.

"Mr. Jensen?" Mrs. Trees asked from her doorway.

"Yes, ma'am."

"Come right in." She looked at Luke. "You too, Luke." She pointed at Sam. "You stay there."

Sam slumped back to the bench as the door shut. This was ridiculous. She needed to get something for her article, something that didn't include bashing her friends.

A virus. That's where she should start. That's what the IT team said it was ... a virus.

Sam pulled her iPhone out of her backpack, thankful they could have cell phones on campus as long as they were kept in lockers during the school day. She started to call Makayla, then remembered that Mac had karate. Instead, Sam sent a message:

Tell me everything you know about computer viruses.

Neither Felicia nor Luke were computer whizzes, so creating a virus was really beyond their abilities. Sam didn't think that to be mean. She meant it as a way to help. Maybe writing an article that focused on the virus would take the attention off her friends.

She opened Safari on her cell and searched for *grade tampering virus*. There were a lot of search results, but nothing similar to what had happened there.

Was it all a fluke? Non-intentional?

Nah. No way. A computer virus doesn't just come along, even she knew that. A person has to create one, build it from scratch. Why would anyone go to the trouble to create such a virus and use it here if they weren't trying to tamper with at least a grade or two? It didn't make sense to think it a fluke. No, this reeked of deliberate. Especially since it was isolated to their school.

Sam ran another search, this time on *computer virus creators*. The first result page she read stopped her cold. Some of the facts were astonishing to her. Apparently, computer hackers and virus creators weren't in the same category. According to the site, hackers were usually far more sophisticated in their methods than virus creators. The site also burst the myth that virus creators were exceptionally smart. That wasn't true, the site pointed out, continuing to report that someone who writes a virus really doesn't have to have any special coding skills. The page read that anyone with a basic understanding of programming was capable of creating a virus.

Sam bookmarked the site to use as a reference for her article. Maybe Mrs. Trees would give her a statement. And she would need one from Dad too, even if it was his usual *no comment*. Maybe that guy in the suit in there was an IT person. Maybe she could get a statement from him too.

Anything to write an article that would take the heat off her friends.

CHAPTER SIX

D ad, can't you at least offer something? Anything besides your standard *no comment*?" Sam had waited until they'd finished dinner to broach the subject of a comment for her article. "I mean, even the IT guy gave me something."

"That's his choice, not mine." Dad leaned back in his recliner and reached for the newspaper. "I would prefer no one give any comments to any press, but obviously I can't control that."

"Come on, Dad. Give me something."

Dad's face was set in stone as he lifted the paper, opening it with a loud *pop*. Sam looked at her mother for help.

Mom shot her a pointed look. "Maybe you're asking the wrong questions, my girl."

Sam tapped the edge of her iPhone case and looked down at the open ISaidWhat?! app. What did Mom mean, *asking the wrong questions*? She needed something for the article from the police. Dad was close-mouthed about the case. She wanted to show how serious this was. How —

She touched the screen to start recording. "Dad, what are some of the legal consequences for whoever is responsible for this?"

Mom smiled and nodded.

Dad lowered the newspaper to his lap, shooting Mom his bulldog look. "Well, it can vary. Charges can include conspiracy to commit theft, conspiracy to commit computer tampering, conspiracy to commit computer trespass, burglary, forgery, computer tampering, theft, and receiving stolen property. A lot of consideration goes into the actual charges, based on the actual crime and intent of the person or persons responsible."

"In this case, what would you expect the charges to be?" Sam began absentmindedly braiding her hair over her left shoulder.

"It's too early to say for sure, but at the moment we're looking at violations of computer tampering, computer trespass, and likely forgery." Dad gave her a smile. "And that's all I can tell you." He lifted the paper, again blocking her view of him.

Well, it was better than nothing. She cut off the

recording, grabbed her cell, and stood. "Thanks, Dad and Mom." She headed to her bedroom.

"Let Chewy back in. It's in the twenties out there," Mom called.

Sam detoured to the kitchen and opened the back door. Chewy darted inside and danced around Sam's legs as she made her way to the bedroom.

She opened a blank blog post document and began typing.

Getting our report cards straightened out might take longer than we'd hoped. That's the news from the district's Information Technology team. Mr. Alexander, one of the Pulaski County Special School District's IT team members, was at our school, investigating the issue with our grades.

"We have looked into the issue and at this time, have determined that a grade tampering virus is to blame. This virus is contained entirely at Joe T. Robinson Middle School. No other schools in the district have been affected," Mr. Alexander told us.

Our principal, Mrs. Trees, had no comment regarding the investigation into who might be responsible for this virus. Detective Sanderson, who is overseeing the investigation on behalf of the Little Rock Police Department, says the culprit could be charged with violations of computer tampering, computer trespass, and likely forgery in this case, but that additional charges such as conspiracy to commit theft, conspiracy to commit computer tampering, conspiracy to commit computer

trespass, burglary, theft, and receiving stolen property
could be included.

Many of us think of those who create viruses to be computer hackers, but research shows that isn't so. Statistics
prove hackers are usually far more sophisticated in their
methods than virus creators. Many of us think virus
creators have to be exceptionally smart. That, too, isn't
true, as reports show anyone with a basic understanding
of programming could be capable of creating a virus.

Even more astounding is the statistical age of many virus
creators. It's a fact that grade-school kids and teens
can write viruses and often do to experiment with their
growing computer skills. As one online security company
reports, most virus creators are men and boys under 30.

What do you think, Senators? Should whoever is responsible for this be charged with an actual crime? Sound off,
Senators, and leave a comment as to what YOU think
should happen to the person or persons responsible.
~ Sam Sanderson reporting.

Sam popped her knuckles and re-read her article.
She did a little tweaking, then sent it to post, and
copied both Mrs. Pape and Aubrey on the email. The
article showed off more of her reporting rather than
using her dad as a source. It still hurt her feelings that
Mrs. Pape didn't stand up for her reporting ability to
Aubrey, instead allowing Aubrey to say she got the story
only because of her dad's connection to the case. Sam
had been doing everything she could think of to prove

her worth as a reporter, but it seemed like she wasn't gaining any ground. How was she supposed to earn the chair of editor next year if everyone believed she only got story assignments because of her father?

Makayla's special ringtone sounded on Sam's cell. Sam punched the speaker feature on. "Hey, how was karate?"

"Brutal. I think *sensei* is trying to do me in." Weariness mixed with excitement in her voice. "But I should be able to go for the black belt this spring."

"That's awesome, Mac. Then you'll really be a ninja."

Makayla laughed. "There is that. So tell me what's going on."

Sam brought Mac up to speed with everything that happened after school in the office, ending with reading her article to her. "What do you think?"

"Your article is good. It makes me think of all the people who could have done this."

"Like?" Mac was on the computer nerd scene, but not because she was a nerd, though she was a computer ninja for sure. If Mac thought someone capable of being able to create a virus, then they were a suspect in Sam's mind.

"I'm not going to go around accusing anyone, Sam."

"I didn't want you to." But if she just gave some names as possibilities . . .

"A lot of people we know could create a virus. Some kids in my computer science class definitely could."

Who was in that class with Mac? "I don't know of any-one who could really do that, aside from you of course."

"Hey, what are you saying?"

Sam laughed. "Nothing. I'm just saying you're the best at computers in our whole school."

"Close," Mac giggled, "but not the best."

"Who's better than you, huh?"

"Doug York, for one. He's the best in my computer science class, hands down."

Doug York. Sam knew who he was all too well. A seventh grader and a horrible whiner. His dad just hap-pened to be a captain with the Little Rock Police, and Sam's dad's boss. Sam didn't hold much respect for Doug because of the way he acted toward her. "You've got to be kidding me. Doug York? He's such a worm."

"I'm serious, Sam, he's scary good."

"He told a bunch of his friends that I'm a brat because I use my dad to get information on my stories, which so isn't true."

"He may be a jerk, but he's brilliant in computer sci-ence." Makayla's voice sounded like she was a bit in awe of him, which said a lot.

"Hmm."

"Sam ... what are you thinking?"

"Well, Doug's always been so whiny and acting like he's so much better than everybody else. If he's capable of creating such a virus, he's exactly the type of person who *would* create it and use it, just because he could."

"That's not fair."

"It is. He'd do it for the attention, just like he does everything else. Talk about a brat."

"Saaaaammmmm."

She wasn't being a very loving neighbor. Sam sighed. "I'm sorry. That was mean." But he did whine a lot and wanted everyone to think he was something special. That wasn't being mean, it was just stating the obvious.

"Better." Makayla chuckled. "Have you heard from Felicia?"

"No, and that worries me. Her mom ... Mac, her mom looked really, really mad. I know she'd been crying."

"Did you ask your dad?"

"I did. He clammed up on me and told me he couldn't tell me anything. Just another way of saying *no comment.*"

"Did you try calling her?"

"I tried a few times before dinner, but it went straight to her voice mail. I left messages. Since she hasn't called back, I'm guessing she's in trouble."

"I feel sorry for her, even though I don't know her that well. Her reputation really made teachers guarded around her. Her attitude when she got here didn't help any, either."

"She was just acting out, Mac."

"I know, I know. You don't have to explain it all to me again. I understand. I'm just saying that's probably how her mom reacts too — assuming the worst because of her past behavior."

"It's unfair. She didn't do this."

"Are you sure, Sam? I'm not saying she's involved, but I'm just asking."

Sam considered Felicia. She came across as tough, but she really had a heart of gold. She was also loyal. She wasn't afraid to bend a rule to the point of breaking. Felicia was nice to Sam, even while trying to act mean and rough. And the girl had a photographic memory, which is why she was able to bring her grades up to a four point in nine weeks' time. Her grades had only dropped at her other school because of the crowd she'd been running with. At least that's what Sam had heard.

"Sam?"

"I'm positive she isn't involved."

"Okay. Then that's good enough for me. Do you have any other suspects?"

"I'm certain Luke Jensen isn't involved, either. Man, have you seen his dad? He's huge. Like a big ole stone wall. Scary."

"You're marking off suspects and not adding any, Sam."

"Well, we can add Doug York."

"Come on. He wouldn't do anything like that."

"Are you sure, Mac? He really despises me. I heard that he wanted to be on the newspaper staff but his dad wouldn't let him. I think he's jealous that I'm on the paper and he isn't."

"Still, to do something like this?" Makayla shook her head. "He's the son of a cop."

Sam shrugged. "So? You know what they say about kids of LEOs, right?"

"LEO?"

"Law Enforcement Officer."

Makayla laughed. "Cute. No, what do they say about LEO's kids?"

"That we're most likely to cross the legal line, or at least go right up to it."

"*You* fit that description to a T."

"Hey now."

"Girl, you've got to admit you push the limits. A lot." Though Sam knew she was kidding, she could sense a hint of seriousness in Makayla's tone.

"Only to get a story." Heat spread across her face.

"That doesn't make it right. Remember, the ends do not justify the means if the means are wrong." More seriousness.

Sam coughed. "Yeah, yeah, yeah. You sound like Dad again. I'm starting to think you might be cut out to be a LEO yourself, Mac."

"Um, no. The thought of handling a gun terrifies me."

Sam burst out laughing.

"What's so funny?"

"You."

"What?"

Sam snorted. "You're scared of a gun, but you love karate, even when it wipes you out. You're a walking contradiction, girl."

"Guns kill people, Sam."

"No, people kill people. Guns are just a vehicle for those types. So are knives. And ropes. And even plastic bags. And yep, even martial arts."

"I'm not going to kill anybody. Stop being morbid."

Sam snorted again. "I didn't say you were. I was just pointing out that people associate guns with violence but not martial arts. Both can be just as deadly."

"True. Guess I never thought about it that way."

"Not to change the subject, but I have a computer question for you."

"Shoot. Pun intended."

Sam grinned. "Goof. Could you go into the school's computer system and see where this virus originated?"

"I can't do that."

"Can't because it's not doable or can't because you won't?"

"Can't because I'm sure the IT team has already tried that."

"You think? Really?"

"Come on, Sam. That's their job."

"But you're brilliant."

Mac laughed. "Of course I am. I'm a computer ninja,

but the IT team would have done that already if they could trace it."

"But could you try?"

"Sam!"

The call-waiting sound rang. Sam glanced at the iPhone. "That's Felicia calling. I'll call you back."

"Can't. I have a bunch of homework. Text me."

"Okay." Sam pressed the button to answer Felicia's call and pressed the phone to her ear. "Felicia?"

"Hey."

"Are you okay? I've been worried about you."

"I'll be fine."

"What happened?"

"Mrs. Trees told my mom that they couldn't ignore the connection between the expulsion from my previous school and the incident with the report cards."

"Oh no."

"Yeah, good ole Mrs. Trees really tried to pin it on me. Asked me the same question about forty different ways, trying to trip me up. But it didn't work because I didn't do it."

"What did your mom say?"

"As you can imagine, she was furious. The IT guy, he helped me out. Asked about our computer at the house, what kind it was and all that. He told Mrs. Trees that he didn't think I could have done it."

"Why?"

"Because our computer here is a PC. He says the

virus had to be created on a Mac so that it wouldn't infect the builder's computer in testing, whatever that means."

That was something she hadn't thought about, but it made sense. "Mac computers don't get viruses that I know of, so it wouldn't be affected by the virus being built on it like a regular PC would." This little fact would sure be in her next article.

"Your dad asked if I had access to any Mac systems. Luckily, I'm not in EAST, so I don't have access."

EAST was a class that focused on student-driven service projects by using teamwork and cutting-edge technology. The EAST classroom had the coolest computers, laptops, software, and accessories, including GPS/GIS mapping tools, architectural and CAD design software, 3D animation suites, virtual reality development, and more. The kids in EAST could identify problems in the community and then use these tools to develop solutions, usually working with other groups. The classroom also had several Mac computers.

"So you aren't in trouble with your mom?"

"She's not happy, but she finally believes I'm not involved. She had to give me the lecture called 'this is a prime example of why I need to be careful of what I do because what we do in the past comes back to haunt us.' In that tone too. You know, all that parent stuff."

Sam nodded, smiling at Felicia's high-pitched and

dramatic impression of her mom. "Yeah, I know, but I'm glad she's not mad at you."

"At first, she wanted to pull me from everything again, but I argued that it would be punishing me for something I didn't do. It was the first time in a long time that we've been able to disagree and come to a compromise without yelling and slamming doors."

Sam cringed. She got mad at her parents all right, what kid doesn't, but they didn't yell. "What's your compromise?"

"Along with keeping my grades up and staying out of trouble, I agreed to join the tutoring team."

"That's actually fun. My best friend did that the last nine weeks and liked it. I bet you'll have fun with it."

"Yeah. I hope so. Anyway, I've got to go. I told Mom I'd only be a few minutes, but I wanted to call you back."

"Okay. I'll see you tomorrow at school."

"Yeah. Oh, and do-gooder?"

"Yeah?"

"Thanks for calling to check up on me." The call disconnected before Sam could say anything in reply.

Sam set down the phone, smiling. She was determined to find out who was responsible for the virus so Felicia wouldn't be under Mrs. Trees' cloud of suspicion for a moment longer.

But where to start? Makayla was right, she had run out of suspects.

Sam leaned back in her chair, rubbed her feet against Chewy's warm belly, and closed her eyes. She let Chewy's fur soothe her.

But she didn't relax for long. A thought occurred to her and she sat upright and opened her eyes in one sudden movement. Makayla had said she was sure the IT team tried to trace the virus. But they obviously hadn't traced it since they didn't seem to have an idea where the virus began. Maybe they weren't as good as Mac thought.

Sam opened the search window on her iMac and typed in: *Alexander* AND *PCSSD IT.*

Maybe the IT guy wasn't so great. If she could just find something that would question his abilities, maybe she could talk Makayla into running the trace herself.

CHAPTER SEVEN

I can't tell you, Sam." She knew that bulldog look — eyebrows drawn down, lips puckered tight — Dad wasn't going to tell her a thing.

She'd try anyway. "Come on, Dad. I know you check out everybody involved in a case. Tell me about Mr. Alexander."

"Why would you think I check out everybody?" He glanced at her for a moment, then went right back to focusing on the road as he drove her to school.

"Because that's just how you are."

"I don't always do that."

"Daaaaad, come on. Tell me about Mr. Alexander."

"He heads up the computer team for your school district."

"Seriously, Dad?" She popped her head back on the

seat of the truck and stared out the window. Why was Dad such a hardnose about the investigation? Mrs. Pape and Aubrey were so wrong in assigning her the case because they assumed she could use her dad as a source — he would probably open up more to someone else. "Can you at least confirm his qualifications?"

"Sam, even if I did know something, I couldn't share that information. You know that." His tone was softer, but that didn't help her mood any.

"Why didn't you tell me he said the virus was created on a Mac?"

"How do you know that? Were you eavesdropping, Sam?" He'd been on her several times about eavesdropping.

"I can't tell you my sources. You know that." Her smugness felt good. For a moment.

"You'd better straighten up your attitude. I know reporting is important to you, but if you are disrespectful, you will be punished."

He was right, but she didn't have to like it.

Dad sighed again as he pulled into her school's lot. "I guess your friend told you about the Mac. Since when did you and Felicia become friends anyway? I haven't heard you mention her."

Sam undid her seatbelt and grabbed her backpack. "She transferred in last nine weeks. I like her. Everyone assumes she's bad, but she's really a good person." She reached for the door handle, then paused. "She didn't have anything to do with this."

"I know, pumpkin." He smiled. "Have a good day. If I can't pick you up after cheer practice, Mrs. Willis will be here." Mom had left this morning to go on assignment for a breaking story in New York. She'd be gone most of the week.

Sam leaned over and kissed his cheek. "Bye, Dad." She shut the door to his truck, then jogged to the cafeteria. The wind was biting cold. She should've worn the scarf Mom had given her for Christmas.

The heat was on full blast in the cafeteria. Sam looked around for Makayla and didn't see her. Her bus must not have arrived yet. Maybe she could find out something while she waited. Sam left the warmth of the building to rush down the breezeway to the main office. She opted to cut through the guidance counselor's office on her way just to get out of the cold. Sam had just passed Mrs. Creegle's door when she heard Mrs. Trees' voice curling down the hall.

Sam froze. She shouldn't eavesdrop, especially considering her conversation with Dad just a few minutes ago, but was it really eavesdropping if she just stood in the middle of an empty office?

"How long is that going to take? I have parents and students alike calling me all day, wanting to know when the issue will be resolved and when the correct report cards will be sent home." Mrs. Trees' voice got shriller.

Sam stood perfectly still, even holding her breath, but she couldn't hear anyone else.

"I understand you're doing everything you can, but you need to understand that I need an estimate of when everything will be fixed. I can't just keep putting off parents."

The school secretary's muffled voice drifted from the front desk. The office door opened and shut. The heater chased darts of cold air down the hallway.

"Well perhaps you should consider hiring someone else to assist in the investigation if you aren't getting timely, satisfactory results. Parents are tired of hearing my same response."

Sam shifted her weight and adjusted her backpack.

"I'm sure you are getting some calls. Imagine how many more you'll be getting when I have nothing new to tell these parents when they call me."

Wow, Mrs. Trees' voice was as shrill as Sam had ever heard.

"You do that, Mr. Alexander. In the meantime, I'll just direct the calls to the district office." A clattering echoed throughout the office, followed by Mrs. Trees' mumbling.

Now probably wasn't the best time to ask the principal anything.

Sam turned and went back through the entrance of the counselor's office. She pushed the door, and it swung wide open so fast that she lost her balance. She reached out to steady herself and ran smack into Officer Bill.

"Whoa there. Where's the fire?"

"Sorry. I'm just heading to the cafeteria to wait for the bell." She could only hope he didn't ask her what she'd been doing. "Bye." She took off.

"Slow it down, young lady. No running," he called after her.

"Yes, sir," she called back, walking at the fastest pace she could until she stepped back inside the cafeteria.

Makayla waved her over. "Why are you so late?"

"Not late. I went to the office to see if I could get some information from Mrs. Trees about the IT guy."

"And?"

"I didn't get to talk to her. She was on the phone, but I don't think they're any closer to fixing the problem."

"Were you eavesdropping?"

"Okay, it's starting to bother me how much you sound like my dad these days. Is he brainwashing you or something?"

Makayla wrinkled her nose. "Don't avoid the question. You were eavesdropping."

"I was standing in the middle of Mrs. Davies' office. That's hardly sneaking around and eavesdropping." Mrs. Davies was the counselor's secretary and an all-around great person. She dressed up in a turkey costume every year to promote the turkey trot fundraiser and didn't seem to mind people laughing as she acted silly to get donations.

"You were listening," Makayla admonished.

Sam shrugged. "I can't help that Mrs. Trees talked so loud that it was impossible not to overhear."

Grinning, Makayla shook her head. "So what'd you learn?"

"That they aren't any closer to getting the problem fixed. Mrs. Trees was quite upset they haven't made more progress. She's getting a lot of calls from parents, and from what I heard, I'm betting she's going to start directing them to the district office."

"They should have made some progress by now." Makayla licked her bottom lip, a true sign of her nervousness.

"Mac, you could go into the system and look around." Sam smiled sheepishly.

"Oh, no. I'm not getting in the middle of this one." She lifted her hands in mock surrender.

"Come on. You wouldn't *do* anything, just look around. See if you can find something to help the IT team."

"News flash, the IT team people are professionals. I'm a student."

"Didn't you read my article that a lot of virus creators are tweens and teens? And from what I could find out about Mr. Ben Alexander, he doesn't have any degrees that would make him a professional."

"You dug into the IT guy?"

"Of course. Even I figured they should've made some progress by now. That they haven't . . . well, it concerns me. Doesn't it concern you? Of course it does. Your face said it all when I told you they weren't closer to fixing the problem."

"But that doesn't mean it's one of the IT guys' fault."

"No? Then whose?"

"I don't know."

"Come on, please help."

"And if I did find something? What would I say, Sam? *Oh, by the way, I was just digging around in something I had no business being in, but I found the answer to your problem.* Yeah, I can so see that happening."

"Mrs. Trees would be so excited to have her problem fixed, I doubt she'd care."

"Really? I don't think so."

"Why not?"

Makayla shook her head. "Think about it. If a student, any student, comes up with anything about the problem, don't you think Mrs. Trees and the rest of the administration and district would think that student was involved with the virus in the first place?"

Oh. Right. Sam hadn't considered that.

"And if I did go into the system and found nothing, I

still might get caught because they probably have extra security now."

Sam kicked at her backpack. "I don't think so. They haven't shut down access to the system in EAST, right? And they haven't shut down the paper's either. We're all on a shared network, so if they changed access, those computers would have been denied."

"True." Makayla frowned. "Why didn't they?"

Sam tilted her head.

"Think about it." Makayla leaned forward. "A virus has infected our school's system ... only *our* school's system. They apparently can't find the point of origin, and have no real suspects as far as we know. The system is still compromised, yet they haven't shut down the most basic of computer operations as a security measure. Why not?"

Sam nodded. "That's what I'm talking about. None of this adds up."

"It does seem a bit ... off."

"Yeah. You'd think the first thing they would've done was to cut off access while they're looking into things. Right?"

"I would say, but maybe they've done something we don't know about."

"Like what?" Sam didn't think they were über smart like that.

"Maybe IT put keyloggers on the system's accessible computers."

Sam tapped her bottom lip, thinking. "You think they put devices on all the computers to log everyone's keystrokes? Why?"

"To get passwords?"

Sam shook her head. "I'm not following you, Mac."

"What if they're keeping information from us, information that they do have a lead?" Makayla's words came out almost on top of each other. "What if they know the point of origin, but are playing dumb so whoever set the virus loose thinks they've gotten away with it?"

Sam wrinkled her nose. "For what purpose?"

"Well, if the computer was one of the ones here, there are a lot of students who use them. A lot. So they'd need to figure out who used that particular computer. If they had the login, but didn't know who it belonged to, a keylogger would help them figure it out. They record not just keystrokes, but can also be programmed to record timestamps of usage."

"There you go with that ninja computer genius stuff again." And Makayla had certainly made a good argument. It was entirely possible there *was* a lead.

Makayla smiled. "Not really. I learned it in the computer research demographic group. You know, you can still change your mind and join. You'd learn a lot."

"No thanks. I have plenty on my plate with the newspaper and cheerleading. Speaking of, are you coming to the basketball game tomorrow?"

"Can't. Karate, remember?"

Sam stuck her bottom lip out. "Can't you skip and come to the game? You never see me cheer anymore except at pep rallies."

"Skip cheering and come watch my karate practice."

Sam grinned and waggled her eyebrows, falling into their familiar old argument. "That's just practice. Besides, everyone knows that karate isn't a real sport or anything."

"Oh and cheerleading is?" Mac grinned back, putting her hands on her hips.

Sam couldn't stop it — she burst out laughing. Little Makayla looking all tough with her hands on her hips. "You make me laugh, Mac."

"Yeah. Whatever."

The bell rang and kids rushed through the cafeteria doors. Blasts of frigid air snaked around them. Sam shivered as she and Makayla walk-ran to their lockers.

"It's so cold my fingers won't work on my lock," Sam said, blowing on her hands.

"Why aren't you wearing gloves, silly?" Makayla reached over and spun Sam's lock, then popped it open.

"Forgot them. And my scarf too."

Makayla shook her head as she pulled out books. "You easily forget anything unless it has to do with reporting."

"Hey! I can't help that's where my passion is."

"Yeah, well your passion better get to moving to English class or Mrs. Beach will write you up."

"Right. See you at lunch." Sam slammed her locker shut and raced to the classroom. She stepped inside a good full minute before the bell rang.

"Hi, Sam." Grace slid into the desk behind Sam.

"Hey, Grace."

"Did you hear about Luke Jensen?"

What, was Grace on Luke patrol? "You mean besides being called to the principal's office yesterday?"

"He has a broken arm."

Sam's jaw dropped. "What?" *Ohmygummybears,* what had happened?

"I heard he broke it at basketball practice yesterday."

That couldn't be. Luke hadn't been at basketball practice yesterday. He'd been in the office. "Where'd you hear that?"

Grace shrugged. "Around."

"How do you know he broke his arm?"

"I saw him this morning. We ride the same bus. He has a blue cast and everything."

Mrs. Beach cleared her throat and began to take attendance.

Sam turned around in her seat and pulled out her notebook, but she was lost in thought. Luke had been fine yesterday afternoon, even if he did look really upset. She'd watched him get into the car with his dad, who looked mad.

A thought ripped around her mind that knotted in her stomach.

**Had Luke's dad been angry enough to hurt him?
Mad enough to break Luke's arm?**

CHAPTER EIGHT

A broken arm did not take away from Luke Jensen's charm. He still wore his award-winning smile and made Sam feel like English wasn't her first language. Kids stopped by his table at lunch, scrawling their signatures in Sharpie on his blue cast.

"Are you going to sign his cast?" Makayla asked, snatching Sam's attention.

"Uh, no." Sam finished drinking her milk and hoped her face wasn't too red. "I'm wondering how he broke his arm."

"I heard he was horsing around with some guys and he fell on it," Lana said as she plopped her tray onto the table on the other side of Sam. "What *is* this? Is it supposed to be a taco or burrito?"

"Who knows? That's why I bring my lunch." To emphasize her point, Makayla shoved a grape in her mouth.

"You bring your lunch because you're a food freak." Sam pointed at her best friend's lunch. "Grapes, lettuce, carrots, and broccoli. All raw and without ranch dressing. That's not a lunch, that's rabbit food."

Makayla grinned and bit off a broccoli stem.

"That's really gross," Sam said, hurrying to finish her lunch. They always ate rather fast so they could go outside for a bit until the bell rang.

"I think I'll take my chances on the taco-burrito whatever." Lana took a big bite of the tortilla wrapped mystery food. She chewed slowly, then swallowed. "Soft taco."

Makayla shook her head. "All processed foods. Probably not even an eighth of an ounce of real food in there."

"Tastes good, though." Lana took another bite.

Sam grinned and looked across the cafeteria and locked stares with Luke. Her heart stuttered.

A long moment passed.

He smiled.

She smiled back.

He gave a little wave.

She waved back.

"Oh, y'all are too cute," Lana said.

Heat flamed on Sam's face. "What?"

"You and Luke. Y'all like each other."

"We do not." Sam's face burned hotter than ever.

"Oh, okay." Lana smiled.

Sam swallowed against a massive boulder in the back of her throat. She quickly grabbed her tray and headed to the trash can.

Aubrey Damas stepped in front of her, and her best friend, Nikki Cole, stood beside her. "Samantha, Mrs. Pape wants to see you." She glanced over at the table where Makayla and Lana waited. "Unless, of course, you're too busy playing with your friends."

One. Love your neighbor as yourself. Two. She's just trying to irritate me, don't take the bait. Three. Love your neighbor as yourself. Four. She probably acts so mean because she's hurting. Five. Love your neighbor — Wait. She might be hurting? Yeah, that would make a lot of sense.

"*Samantha*, are you listening? Hello? Are you in there?" Aubrey pointed at Sam's head. "Anybody home up there?"

"Aubrey, stop. You're just being mean," Nikki said.

Aubrey turned, glaring at her best friend. "Are you really sticking up for her?"

"I'll head over to Mrs. Pape's room now. Are you coming?" Sam stepped in, ignoring Aubrey's meanness and sharp tongue.

"Of course I'm coming. I came all the way here to get you, didn't I?"

"Then let's go." Sam gave Makayla and Lana a slight wave, then led the way out of the cafeteria, Aubrey and Nikki trailing behind her.

They walked along the cold breezeway in silence, something Sam could appreciate when it came to Aubrey. But maybe she'd hit on a reason why Aubrey was so bitter. It was possible she was lashing out because her feelings had been hurt. And they must have been hurt pretty bad for Aubrey to act like she did all the time. What would cause that? Maybe she should go out of her way to be nice to Aubrey. Maybe that's what her resolution of loving her neighbor was really all about.

"Could you hurry it up, Samantha? I'm freezing," Aubrey said, right on her heels.

Then again, maybe her resolution had nothing to do with Aubrey.

She opened the door to Mrs. Pape's classroom. This was the eighth grade English teacher's planning period. "Hi, Sam. Come on in."

Sam blew on her freezing hands as she took a seat in one of the pulled out chairs.

"You're getting quite a lot of hits on your article."

"I checked before I came to school and there were about twenty."

"There are currently five hundred and sixty-two."

Sam's eyes bugged. "What?"

Mrs. Pape smiled. "It's one of the highest responses we've had in quite some time. Good work."

Sam couldn't stop her wide smile. "Thanks."

"Now, there are a lot of comments in support of you and your reporting," Mrs. Pape began, "and there are plenty of comments that are just sounding off as you asked."

Where was she going with this?

"But there are also some comments that sound like there could be an agenda of some sort."

"An agenda?"

Aubrey rolled her eyes. "You know, comments that seem like they might have come from someone involved in the whole deal."

"We're not saying everyone who comments is a suspect," Mrs. Pape interrupted, "but to employ due diligence, we should follow up on them."

"That's a directive from the principal." Aubrey looked smugger than usual, if that was possible.

"I thought she had other suspects," Sam said, thinking of both Felicia and Luke.

"She's trying to be very thorough." Mrs. Pape smiled. "So, we need to make a list of the people who commented who come across as being in support of this virus."

"Isn't that kinda like profiling?" Sam had heard her dad and his partner discussing the pros and cons of profiling — lumping a group of people together based upon something in common like race or profession ... or being in support of something or someone. She still wasn't sure which way her dad leaned on the subject of profiling. She wasn't sure how *she* felt about it.

"No. We're just perusing commenters to see if something jumps out at us. You know, someone who appears to be a little too much in support of the virus and its results. We're just helping the investigation. Sam, you go through comments one through two hundred. I'll go through two hundred and one through four hundred. Aubrey, you go through four hundred and one through the end."

Uh-huh. "Okay." Sam moved to sit behind a computer terminal. She opened the blog and began to scroll through the comments.

As Mrs. Pape said, some comments were just *good job* notes to Sam on the actual article. Then there were the comments from parents and others who just wanted to get the system straightened out. Sam passed those by. She stopped on comment number forty-one and reread it.

> **The mess up isn't a crime committed by someone. The crime is that someone was able to cause the mess. School administrators are to blame.**

Sam looked at the poster's screen name: Robinson-Radar. She wrote it down on her list, then continued reading. Comment number sixty-eight made her stop.

A crime? You've got to be kidding me. Crimes are murders, rapes, and assaults. Grade tampering? Not hardly. Whoever's responsible should get an A for being able to hack into the computer system. I say put them on honor roll.

Sam added SickofSchoolStuff to her list, then went back to reading. She'd made it to number one hundred and ninety-three before she stopped again. This comment seemed especially brutal.

School and district should learn to lock down their own systems. I bet their payroll system is still functioning just fine. Keep paying the idiots who let the virus in, but let's penalize the students by holding their grades hostage. Yeah, that makes so much sense.

Sam listed RagOnRobinson to her list just as the bell sounded. She handed her list to Mrs. Pape. "All done."

"Thanks, Sam. See you in class."

"What are you going to do with that list, Mrs. Pape?"

"Turn it in to Mrs. Trees." Mrs. Pape smiled. "Don't worry, she'll investigate everything thoroughly. Now hurry up so you aren't late to class."

Sam rushed to her locker, where she met Makayla. "What'd Mrs. Pape want?"

After telling Makayla about the list of people who commented, Sam shut her locker and leaned against it. "Some of those comments were pretty vicious. I hate that Mrs. Trees is going to find out who they are. It's almost like they're getting in trouble for enacting their freedom of speech. That's not right."

Makayla shrugged. "They're probably just turning the list over to your dad and letting the police do the tracking. You haven't violated their rights or anything. Mrs. Trees could find the names herself. You just helped her sort through them."

"I still feel awful. Like I'm snitching on someone."

"If those people didn't want to be questioned, they wouldn't have left a comment."

"Do you think the person who created the virus is one of the people who posted?"

"I don't know." She paused. "I don't even know if the person who created the virus is the one who infected the system."

Sam stopped. "What are you saying? You think there's more than one person involved?"

"It's possible, isn't it?" Makayla shut her locker. "But that's not for us to figure out. Mrs. Trees will turn it over to someone else to look into it."

"I hope they don't turn it over to Mr. Alexander. He'd never figure it out."

Makayla frowned. "That's not nice, Sam."

"Come on, Mac. You know it's true."

"Maybe. Hey, I can't be late. I'll catch you after school."

"Nope. I have cheer practice."

"Call me later then." Makayla rushed off.

Sam headed down to the EAST classroom. Mrs. Shine smiled as she entered. "Hello, Sam."

"Hi, Mrs. Shine." It was obvious to everyone that Sam was Mrs. Shine's teacher's pet. The feeling was mutual, as Mrs. Shine was one of Sam's favorite teachers.

She took her seat in front of one of the iMacs and pulled out her notebook with her project notes. She'd been working on the Historical Fitness Trail since last year. She'd originally had a partner, but Anna had moved away, leaving Sam to finish the project on her own. She didn't mind. It gave her time to think as well as get the work done the way she wanted it.

And Makayla called her a control freak.

Smiling to herself, Sam logged into the computer. Her thoughts drifted back to what Makayla had said. Was it possible two people were involved? One who created the virus and the other who put it in the system? Had her dad considered that? Was that why he was being so closed-mouthed about the whole investigation?

Sam thought about the articles she'd read about grade tampering.

"Hey, Sam?" Marcus Robertson, the newspaper's eighth grade photographer stopped at her desk. "Did you hear about the PTO meeting last night?"

Neither of her parents belonged to the parent teacher organization. "No. What's up?"

"They voted to let us have a winter formal this year."

"Really?" How had she not heard this all day? A winter formal could be fun. She and Makayla and Lana and some of the cheerleaders always had fun at the school dances.

"Yeah. For Valentine's Day."

Ugh — scratch that plan. Romantic stuff. For most dances, groups of friends would get together and go. Mostly, the groups of girls danced and the boys hung out along the wall talking about football or basketball, depending on the season. But for a Valentine's Day dance ... that would be different.

"Yeah. Anyway, I was wondering ..."

If he asked her to go with him, she'd fall out. They were friends. If he ruined that by asking her to go to the dance with him, she'd —

"Do you think Frannie would go with me if I asked her?"

Ooh. "Frannie?"

He blushed. "Yeah. I mean, she asked me to be her escort for homecoming and all. She's really pretty and ..." Even his ears turned pink. "I know you cheerleaders hang out a lot and talk. I was just wondering if you thought she'd go with me if I asked her."

Awkward. "I, uh, I really don't know, Marcus." What was she supposed to say? She wanted to tell him to figure it out himself, but that wouldn't be loving her neighbor, now would it? "I know she thinks you're sweet." She'd heard Frannie say that.

"Really?" His eyes lit up almost like Chewy's when Sam dangled bacon over the dog's nose.

"Yeah. Really. So maybe you should talk to her, huh?" That's the best she could do. Non-committal in case Frannie wasn't interested.

"I will." He took a step away from her desk, then stopped and turned back to her. "Thanks, Sam."

She waited until he was back at his desk before twisting her hair into a loose ponytail and staring at her project notes on the computer. She grabbed a pen and stuck it in her wound-up hair to secure it at the base of her neck, but her finger slipped and she dropped the pen. It hit the side of the keyboard, then rolled under the monitor.

Sam shook her hair free and bent to pick up the pen. And that's when she saw it — a little device much like a USB jump drive — sticking into the computer's tower sitting under the desk.

She leaned closer, realizing what she was looking at. Just like Makayla had suggested.

It was a keylogger device.

CHAPTER NINE

Nikki will cover the upcoming dance and Kevin will report on the basketball game this Friday night." Big surprise. Everybody knew Aubrey had a crush on Kevin Haynes and gave him the best assignments.

Aubrey glanced at her clipboard. "Samantha will stay on the report card fiasco since her dad is over the investigation." She set the clipboard on her desk. "That's all."

Sam frowned. How many times did Aubrey have to bring up Sam's dad? Hadn't she proven herself a worthy reporter on her own merit? Probably not ever to Aubrey.

Felecia leaned over. "She's just saying that because she's jealous of you and intimidated by your talent. Don't let her get to you." She lowered her voice to a whisper. "Or at least don't let it show that she's getting to you."

"Hey, Sam?"

She spun in her seat to face a dimple-flashing Luke Jensen. *Ohmygummybears!* Why did he always make her feel like a blubbering idiot? "Yeah?"

"Can I talk to you for a second?" He glanced at Felicia and Lana. "Alone?"

"Sure." Sam shoved to her feet and knocked her chair over. Heat flooded her face as she bent to straighten the chair, then stepped away from her friends. What if he was going to ask her to the dance? Her pulse went into overdrive.

Worse, what if he was going to ask her if he should ask someone else like Marcus did? Man, she didn't think she could handle that one with a straight face. "Yeah?"

"Listen, I wanted to thank you for not saying anything yesterday to your dad. You know, about why I was in the office."

"What happened?"

"I told them that my proposed project was all connected to sports and I had no idea why Mr. Emmitt thought it could be connected to the report cards problem. I think I convinced Mrs. Trees that I hadn't completed the finished project yet."

"That's good." She glanced at his cast. "What about your dad? Did you convince him?"

He dropped his stare to the floor. "Yeah, but he was still upset because I hadn't finished the project. He's always on me not to wait until the last minute."

"How'd you break your arm?"

"Oh." He lifted his cast and gave her a sheepish smile. "Me and Mark were wrestling around and I fell on the coffee table. Guess I won't be playing in the game Friday night."

Wrestling? Was that just a cover-up story? Sam couldn't tell. "That's too bad. Does it hurt a lot?"

He shrugged. "Not so much now. Hurt pretty bad last night, but the pain medication the doctor gave me makes it better. Bearable." He smiled, flashing those dimples at her.

It was entirely possible she was looking for something that wasn't there about his dad and his broken arm. That's what Dad told her all the time, that her suspicious mind was in permanent overdrive.

"Anyway, just wanted to say thanks for keeping my secret."

"Sure. No problem." She went back to her seat between Felicia and Lana.

"Did he ask you to the dance?" Lana asked.

Heat filled her face again. "No, of course not. We're just friends." Sam concentrated on getting her pen out of her backpack. Slowly.

"He's gonna ask you. I can tell that he likes you." Lana grinned.

"Shut up." Sam gave her friend a gentle nudge. "Don't you have a teacher spotlight article to write?"

"Okay, okay. I'll leave it be." Lana moved up to the

next row of tables and brought one of the two computers sitting there out of sleep mode.

The hairs on the back of Sam's neck rose. She lifted her head and caught Luke staring at her. She froze. He smiled. She smiled back. He turned back to talk with Kevin Haynes and Tam Lee.

"I need to talk to Mrs. Pape. I'll be back in a minute," Felicia said before moving to the teacher's desk.

Sam let out a slow breath, then remembered about the keylogger device in EAST. She needed to see if the paper's computers had any keyloggers too. She pulled one of the all-in-one Hewlett Packard systems on the table toward her, turning it slightly.

Yep, sure enough, there was a small device in the computer's USB jump drive slot on the side of the machine. They were logging the keystrokes here too. And if they had keyloggers on the EAST computers and the newspaper's, then they most likely had them in the media center's computers as well.

This meant they probably *did* know that the point of origin of the virus infection came from within the school. That would be most obvious, of course, but it was possible for someone to hack into the system by way of a network connection. Makayla had done it before, so another computer ninja genius could do it too. Sam could probably do it if she had enough time, inclination, and did a little research.

But who had installed the keyloggers? The police? Mrs. Trees? Mr. Alexander?

A chilling thought hit her. What if the person who put the virus into the system had installed the keyloggers before the virus had been installed? What if that's how they got into the system — they used someone else's login information?

A totally innocent person could end up taking the blame.

How could she figure out how long the devices had been in the computers? Surely there was a way to tell. Makayla would be able to figure it out, Sam was sure.

If the keyloggers belonged to the culprits, should she tell her dad so they could dust them for fingerprints?

"Sam?"

Sam jumped and turned to face Nikki Cole.

"Sorry, didn't mean to startle you."

"It's okay. I was lost in thought." Sam glanced around the room for Aubrey, but didn't see her. "What's up?"

"I want to apologize for the way Aubrey treats you."

Sam grinned. "She's been that way ever since I got to middle school. It's not your fault."

"Well, actually, it kind of is."

Sam crinkled her nose. "How do you figure that?"

"When you were helping me with the whole bullying thing, I think Aubrey got a little jealous that I confided in you."

A few months ago, Nikki's younger brother, Jefferson, had realized that if he or Nikki needed attention, their parents, who were separated, would put aside their differences to be there for Nikki or Jefferson. Her brother had taken it a step too far and began anonymously bullying Nikki. Sam had helped uncover the truth.

"Isn't that kind of her own fault, since she avoided you during that time?" Sam asked. Nikki had been nominated to homecoming court, and Aubrey hadn't.

"It is, but you know Aubrey . . . she doesn't see it as her fault in any way."

"Of course she doesn't. She never does." Sam laughed. "It's okay, Nikki. I'm pretty much used to it. She doesn't get to me much anymore. I let her remarks just roll off my back."

At least most of the time.

"I know, but I just wanted to let you know I was sorry for being part of her meanness before."

"Thanks. I appreciate that."

"Nikki!" Aubrey called from the doorway.

Sam grinned. "Speak of the devil . . . you'd better go before she gets in a huff."

Nikki smiled. "Thanks." She joined Aubrey at the editor's desk.

The desk Sam was determined to have next year, which meant she needed to get cracking on an article for tomorrow. A really good one.

● ● ●

"Come on girls, jog it out." Mrs. Holt, the cheerleading sponsor, clapped as they got off the gym floor after stretching and began to jog around the basketball court.

"Don't know why we're bothering. It's supposed to sleet and snow on Friday so you know they'll cancel the game," Remy Tucker, co-captain of the squad and homecoming queen, said as she led the team.

"They'll probably cancel school too," Bella, the perky blond cheerleader, added.

"I hope they cancel school," Kate said. "We've only been back three days and already I'm sick of all the drama." She rolled her eyes and waggled her eyebrows.

Missy, the other co-captain, laughed. "How can you be sick of drama, Kate? You're the one who brings on all the drama." She took off running, passing Remy and Bella.

Kate took off after her.

"Well, I hope it snows. I love winter." Frannie fell into step beside Sam, matching her pace.

Sam nodded. "I like the winter too, just not the super cold temperatures. I like cold and snow if I have a nice, toasty fire to sit in front of and a cup of hot chocolate to drink." She was rambling, but only because she didn't know if she should mention Marcus's question or not. It wasn't like he asked her not to say anything, but she felt awkward enough as it was.

Maybe he hadn't asked her. What if she said something then he changed his mind? That would make Frannie feel pretty lousy.

"Marcus asked me to the winter formal." Frannie blurted out.

Sam grinned. Guess that meant he didn't change his mind. "What'd you say?"

"I told him I'd love to."

"That's cool." What would she do if Luke asked her? Probably pass smooth out.

Frannie nodded. "Yeah. I made sure he understood that meant I'd meet him there. My dad would freak if he thought I was actually going out with a guy."

Sam grinned bigger. "How do you think I feel? My dad's a cop. He's told my mom that I'm not allowed to even think about dating until I graduate high school."

Frannie's eyes grew rounder. "Is he serious?"

"I don't think so. Mom laughed when he said it." Man, she hoped he wasn't serious. Not that she thought about dating now, since she couldn't get a driver's license, but when she was in high school ... well, dating was definitely worth discussing then.

"Whew."

Sam nodded. "I like Marcus a lot. He's super nice. You two are good for each other, I think."

"I think so too." Frannie blushed under her dark African-American complexion. "There's something else."

"Yeah?" Sam slowed her pace.

"When I was changing in the locker room, when most of y'all were already stretching, I heard Mrs. Holt and Mrs. Christian talking."

Sam slowed to a walk.

Frannie looked around. The other cheerleaders were almost a good eight feet in front of them. Mrs. Holt was looking at a book and Mrs. Christian had the girls' basketball team on the bleachers, talking to them.

She went on. "They were talking about the grades and everything, and Mrs. Christian said the district had a backup of the system from the last day of school before Christmas break. Mrs. Holt asked why hadn't they just restored the system from that backup."

That made sense, and Sam was more than a little disappointed in herself that she hadn't considered a backup. What had she been thinking?

Sam stopped. "What'd Mrs. Christian say?"

"She said they couldn't."

"What?" Sam asked. That made no sense. Everyone knew the point of a backup was to be able to restore something in the event of data loss.

"I don't know anything more than that. They stopped talking when they saw me."

"That just doesn't make sense."

Frannie started walking again. "I don't know what's going on, but since you're covering the case and your dad's over the investigation and all, I thought you should know."

"Thanks, Frannie."

"No problem."

"Sam! Frannie! Get a move on. We're ready to practice our stunts." Mrs. Holt motioned them to their corner of the basketball court while Mrs. Christian led the girls' basketball team to the other side.

As Sam went through the stunt, pyramid, and cheers practice, her mind couldn't stop thinking about what Frannie had overheard.

How come they couldn't restore the system from a backup?

CHAPTER TEN

As soon as cheer practice was over, Sam rushed into the locker room to change. For once she didn't care if her dad was unable to pick her up. Sam would be able to love her neighbor, Mrs. Willis, even if she was hard of hearing and didn't see as well as she used to. Sam grabbed her backpack and headed out into the parking lot.

A cold wind slapped her in the face as soon as she stepped outside. She glanced over the parking lot, shivering, and saw Mrs. Willis's old car parked in the back row, as was usual when she picked Sam up when Sam's dad had to work and her mom was out of town.

"Hello, dear. How was your day?" Mrs. Willis asked as Sam slid into the front seat and blew on her hands.

The cracked vinyl popped as she buckled her

seatbelt. "It was a good day." For the most part. "Thank you for picking me up."

Mrs. Willis started the car, revving the engine like she always did. Sam suspected she needed to do that to make sure the vehicle was running. "It's no problem. I finished making my grocery list while I waited."

Sam knew Mrs. Willis was lonely. Many times, she'd told Sam she left the television or radio on just to hear other voices. Sam felt sorry for her, so the whole way home, she rattled on about her day — cheerleading, school … any and everything — right up until they pulled into Mrs. Willis's driveway next door.

"Thank you again for the ride," Sam shut the passenger door and slung her backpack over her shoulder. "I'm sorry I talked your ear off."

"Dear, I always love hearing about your day. Remember, if you need anything I'm right next door." Mrs. Willis locked the car door and toddled toward her front door. She never used the carport door. Never had, for as long as Sam could remember.

Sam jogged across the yard to her garage door. She punched in the code on the keypad by the door. The mechanical door slowly began to rise. She gave Mrs. Willis a wave goodbye before heading into the house, hitting the button to shut the garage door on her way into the kitchen.

Chewy met her as soon as she walked inside, jumping and wagging her whole body.

Sam laughed, dropped her backpack onto the entry bench and then made her way inside, pausing to love on her dog. Chewy licked her face while standing on her hind legs. The dog was one of Sam's best friends.

Sam let the dog out into the backyard before starting on dinner. This morning before school she'd pulled one of the casseroles from the freezer and shoved it into the refrigerator. That meant it wouldn't take nearly as long to cook, so it should be ready just about the time Dad got home from work.

When Mom was home, Sam helped her make up lots of casseroles that were easy to freeze and store. That way, when Mom was off on a journalist assignment, Sam and her dad always had home-cooked meals.

Tonight was one of those nights, but Mom would be home this weekend.

Chewy barked, and Sam let her back in through the kitchen door.

Sam had just finished dumping the salad mix into the bowls when the front door squeaked open. Dad's keys clanked into the wooden bowl on the entry table. "Hi, Daddy," she called out.

"Hi, pumpkin." As usual, he went immediately to his and Mom's room to lock up his gun and badge.

She added dressing and cheese to the salads, then set them on the placemats on the kitchen table.

"Something smells good." Dad kissed the top of her head as he came into the kitchen.

"It's stuffed bell pepper casserole," Sam answered as she handed him the hot pads.

"No wonder my stomach's growling." He pulled the casserole from the oven and set it on the cooling rack.

Sam turned off the oven and passed him the silver server and two plates. He cut generous pieces of the cheesy, meaty casserole, then carried the plates to the table. Sam joined him, carrying two glasses of milk.

Dad said grace. Her own stomach growling, Sam shoved a bite of the hot casserole into her mouth. The yummy tomato and cheese flavors made her taste buds stand up and dance. She couldn't help making a little sighing sound.

Shaking his head, Dad laughed. "You always enjoy your food. You make the funniest sounds."

"I love food. What can I say?" Sam smiled before taking another bite.

"How was your day?" He pointed at her with his fork. "And don't ruin my dinner by grilling me about the case."

Sam resisted the urge to growl out loud. Her dad could irritate her faster than anyone else in the whole world. "Can't we just discuss it?"

Dad set down his fork. "Off the record?"

"If you tell me it's off the record, then it is." This was her integrity as a reporter.

"Okay, off the record, what do you want to know?"

"Did the police install keylogger devices on the school's computers after the virus was planted?"

"No." But he didn't look surprised.

"Did the IT guys install them?"

"Off the record, yes."

She nodded, tracing the lip of her glass of milk as she thought. "Why haven't they just restored the system back to the point of the last backup?"

He looked surprised that she'd asked. "Mr. Alexander said they can't."

"Why? Was the backup corrupt?" That would mean the virus was planted before they left for Christmas break.

"I'm not sure, but he was pretty adamant it couldn't be done."

"Did you turn that information over to the police department's cyber unit?"

Dad balled his napkin up and set it on his empty plate. "Why do you think it needs to be turned over to our cyber unit?"

"This is just you and me talking, right?" she asked. He nodded.

"Well," she took the last sip of milk and set the empty glass back on the table. "I don't think you should just take Mr. Alexander's word on anything. Something about him is a little off. He doesn't even have a degree in computer science or anything."

"Have you been digging into Mr. Alexander's background?"

She rolled her eyes. "Dad, I'm a reporter. Of course I did research on him. Due diligence and all that, remember?"

Dad chuckled.

"So did you turn it over to your cyber unit?"

"I did, but they haven't had a chance to look at the case. They're backed up from all the hackers who stole credit and debit card information over the holidays." Dad finished off his glass of milk. "What else bothers you about Mr. Alexander?"

"I just find it odd that the school district would hire him as an IT guy if he doesn't even have a computer-based degree. I couldn't find that he had any degree at all. So why is he working for the district if he isn't really qualified?"

"Just because he doesn't have a degree doesn't mean he isn't qualified, pumpkin. There are a lot of important computer geniuses who don't have degrees, like Bill Gates, Steve Jobs, and Mark Zuckerberg."

"I know. And I know about the Thiel Fellowship too."

Dad tented his fingers and rested his elbow on the table. "Um, I'm not familiar with that."

Sam grinned. "The Thiel Fellowship awards one hundred thousand dollars to twenty people under the age of twenty every year so they can skip college to focus on research or a dream."

Dad's eyes widened. "There's a fellowship that pays people not to go to college?"

Sam laughed and nodded. "The fellowship allows the person to focus on research or a dream, like a high-tech project or something meaningful like that."

"That's . . . that's just insane."

"Obviously I'm not applying." Sam laughed.

"I should say not. One hundred thousand dollars sounds like a lot of money, but you can make that in just one year with a college degree. What about year two for those who took the fellowship? They have no guarantee they'll even be employable."

"Or, they could become like Jobs or Gates or Zuckerberg and be wealthy for the rest of their lives."

Dad stood and took his dishes to the sink. "I guess I just don't understand. In this day and age when we put so much stock in education and knowledge, I find it appalling that any entity would actually pay someone not to go to college. It just befuddles my mind."

Sam kept chuckling as she rinsed the dishes and placed them in the dishwasher. "Did you know that David Karp never even got his high school diploma?"

"Should I know who that is?"

Sam shook her head and laughed. "Dad, he's the guy who started Tumblr. He sold it to Yahoo! for like one-point-one billion dollars."

"You're scaring me, Sam." He leaned against the counter.

She bent forward and gave him a hug. "You don't have to sweat it. I'm not a computer genius, and you know I plan to get my journalism degree from Mizzou." She would get a scholarship, get her degree, then become an amazing journalist, just like Mom. Maybe even surpassing Mom.

He kissed the top of her head. "For once, I'm extremely pleased you have your future all mapped out." He popped her softly with the dishtowel. "Now, go do your homework. I'll finish cleaning up the kitchen."

"Okay." She moved toward her bedroom.

"And Sam?"

She turned back to him. "Yes, sir?"

"Don't forget, everything I told you was off the record."

"I won't." She grinned and headed to her room. Chewy followed, prancing alongside Sam as she shut her bedroom door behind her and plopped on the bed.

Sam didn't have any homework so she grabbed her iPhone. Her heart skipped a little beat as she saw the call she'd missed — Luke Jensen! And he'd left a voice mail. She quickly played it back.

"Uh, hi, Sam. This is Luke. Listen, I just wanted to say thanks for not saying anything. I told my dad everything and he's helping me and my brother work on my project, so it's all good right now." A pause sounded on the recording. "Anyway, thanks."

Sam smiled to herself. This was almost better than

him asking her to a silly formal dance. She checked the time. Makayla should be done with dinner by now. She dialed her number and waited for the connection.

"Hey, Sam." Makayla always sounded like she was smiling.

That was okay, because Sam couldn't stop smiling herself. She told her bestie about Luke's call.

"That's so cool," Makayla said. "Did he mention the dance at all?"

"No." Sam admitted to herself she was a little disappointed, but it was okay. She quickly changed the subject. "Tell me why we haven't just restored the system from the backup." Sam lay on her bed, petting Chewy's head. The iPhone set on her chest, the speaker feature turned on.

"Well, hello to you too." But Makayla chuckled. "You must be hot on a lead."

"I am. Sorry."

"I know how you are. No offense taken."

"Good. So give me a reason why we haven't just restored the system from the backup."

"Well, there are several that come to mind. First, the backup is corrupt."

"If it's corrupt, wouldn't that mean the virus got to it, which means that the suspected timeframe is off?"

"Not necessarily. A corrupt backup could have nothing to do with a virus. Sometimes backup servers just glitch because of the enormous amount of data they're

processing every day and because they're writing over
and over the older data."

Sam stopped petting Chewy and tapped her finger-
tips together. "Um, isn't that the whole purpose of a
backup, to actually, I don't know, *back up data*?"

Makayla laughed. "You would think. And usually it
goes off without a hitch, but there are times when hard-
ware needs to be replaced."

"That's kind of reaching, wouldn't you say? Our
backup is corrupt right when we need it?"

"It would be quite the coincidence."

"Yeah, I'm not buying that."

"Okay, if the backup isn't corrupt, then the main reason I think we couldn't use the backup is that the system has been damaged to the point where the backup
couldn't overwrite the virus."

Sam chewed her bottom lip. "Tell me more."

"Well, if a virus has a self-destruct feature, obviously
IT and the police's cyber unit wouldn't want a self-
destruct to be activated. If it was, they wouldn't be able
to study and analyze the virus itself."

"A self-destruct?" Sam sat up and took the phone off
speaker, pressing it against her ear.

"It would automatically locate every bit of the virus'
code, remove it, and write random data over the origi-
nal code, so you couldn't even find a trace of the virus.
Self-destructs are designed to prevent anybody from

studying a particular virus using a computer that's been infected but has received the self-destruct code."

"Every virus has a self-destruct feature?"

"No. Actually, most don't. But if the person who created this virus really wanted to erase every link back to them, they might have built it in. They would have written a module responsible for removing the virus from the compromised system. It's also known as the *uninstaller*. Basically, it tries to leave no traces of the infection behind so no one can trace it or even break it down to find any identifying markers."

"Hmmm." Even though Sam took computer class and knew enough, all of this type of stuff was over her head. "How would they know if there was this self-destruct file in the virus?"

"Someone who knew what they were looking for would have to find it. Most of the self-destruct files are hidden in a restore program. Like, there would be a specific .ocx file embedded in the restore process. So as someone starts the restore process, the .ocx file would be activated, and the self-destruct would launch."

Sam considered who all would have looked at the system. Dad said the cyber unit hadn't had a chance yet, so the hold on restoring wasn't from the police. That meant it had to come from the district's IT team. Mr. Alexander.

Maybe he was better than she'd thought.

Sam ran her fingers through Chewy's fur. "Would an IT team automatically know to look for that?"

"Maybe. I'm not sure the district's IT team would, if that's what you're getting at, and I'm not real sure if they'd want to preserve a virus to study it. If it had a self-destruct, it might have clues as to who the creator was," Makayla said without hesitation.

"Really?" Sam caressed Chewy's soft ear.

"Most virus writers have a certain way of writing code that can identify them. Like, specific colors for the lines of code or something like that. It's usually identifiable because it's usually used more than once. Maybe the police said not to restore from a backup in order to preserve the virus in hopes they could use the code itself to help identify the creator."

But they didn't. "What if I said I knew the police didn't?" Sam asked.

"Your dad told you this?"

"Not on the record."

"Hmm. Well, I'm not real sure then. It doesn't make sense, but since I'm not looking at the code of the virus, I really can't even guess."

Sam stood and paced. Chewy let out a heavy sigh and dropped onto her dog bed beside Sam's desk. "If you could get into the grading program, where the virus is, could you see if it has a self-destruct?" If the virus didn't have a self-destruct, then they could restore from the backup without worry.

CHAPTER TEN

"Probably, but I doubt they'll let me poke around in it," Makayla said with a half snort.

Sam paced faster. "Couldn't you go in remotely and look?"

"Sam! I'm not going in to poke around without permission. No way."

"Just to look. You wouldn't be doing anything."

"No."

"Come on, aren't you the least bit curious? Just to see such a virus code?" Sam stopped pacing and bit her lip. Makayla was curious, especially about computer code and stuff. That's why she'd joined that computer research demographic group. Sam didn't know everything they did, but a lot of it was counter-computer hacking stuff and anti-virus. At least, that's what she thought it was about when Mac had described it.

"If I'm being honest, yes, I am curious," Makayla admitted. "But not enough to break into the system to look at a virus."

"What's the harm?"

"Number one, it's illegal and number two, it could infect my computer."

Sam let out a loud sigh. "It doesn't infect the Mac system. If you wanted, you could even come over and use mine."

"Sam, that doesn't stop it from being illegal."

"But the cyber unit hasn't even had time to look at it. It's just the district's IT team, and you said you

127

SAMANTHA SANDERSON OFF THE RECORD

doubted they would want to study a virus." Sam kept going before Makayla could argue more. "Think about it. Something isn't right. If the IT team isn't planning to preserve the virus and figure it out, then what's the hold up? Why aren't they restoring the system? If the backup tape is corrupt at the exact time we need it, that's too much of a coincidence. You've gotta admit, Mac, something smells fishy."

"Well, it does. You're right on all counts, but I'm not going to go into the system illegally, for any reason."

Sam stopped pacing and gripped her phone tightly. "Come on, Mac."

"No, Sam. I'm not budging on this."

"No one would ever know."

"I'd know, Sam. You'd know. And we both know it's wrong."

Sam flopped down on her bed. No wonder the voice of her conscience sounded remarkably like Mac's voice. Sam knew her bestie wouldn't budge. There had to be another way to figure it out. Mom always said, "Real journalists don't accept closed doors. We find window-ways in."

She just had to find the window-way in.

"Sam, I'm sorry."

"That's okay, Mac. I shouldn't have pushed." It wasn't like she could force Makayla to use her genius ninja computer skills.

Wait a minute . . .

"What if I could get you permission to go in and look? Would you do it then?"

"Permission from whom?" Makayla sounded guarded.

"Either Mrs. Trees or the police?"

"Oh. Yeah. Well, if they said it was okay, then I don't see why not."

Sam smiled. "Okay. I'll see what I can do. I'll talk to Mrs. Trees tomorrow morning."

"Okay. I've gotta go. Chloe needs help with her math." Makayla's little sister wasn't as motivated as Mac to get the highest grades possible.

"See you in the morning." Sam hung up and closed her eyes.

She needed to get permission for Mac to get into the grading program for a couple of reasons: if there was no self-destruct, they could restore the grades from the backup. And, if it did, it might even tell them who the virus creator was.

A window-way in to a scoop of a story. She'd prove she was a good reporter once and for all, even without using her dad as a source.

CHAPTER ELEVEN

*B*uzz! *Buzz! Buzz! Wake up, Sam. Wake up!*
Sam rolled over and slid her finger over her cell's touch screen to turn off the alarm. Chewy jumped up on the bed, wagging her body, doing her little whining thing to get Sam's full attention.

"Okay, okay. I'll let you out." Sam rolled out of bed and immediately shivered.

Chewy bounced up and down on her hind legs.

Sam grinned. "Hang on, girl. Give me a second." She shoved her feet into her big, fluffy Ugg slippers and wrapped a robe around her fleece-y pajamas, slipping her iPhone into the pocket, then headed down the hall to the kitchen.

Dad was on his cell as she passed him at the counter. She opened the kitchen door and Chewy shot outside.

Sam's eyes widened. There had to be at least three or four inches of ice and snow covering the ground. She shut the door and pulled out her phone. Shivering against the chill from just the brief moment she'd had the door open, Sam quickly checked the local news station's site. She let out a whoop as they scrolled through the school closings and she saw the Pulaski County Special School District listed.

At the sound of Sam's shout, Dad turned and walked into the dining room. Oops. Sam grimaced, then headed to the fridge to pull out milk and make a cup of hot chocolate. Snow day! This called for whipped cream.

"Well, keep me updated. Be careful." Dad walked back into the kitchen. "Love you too. Here's Sam." He handed her the phone. "It's Mom."

"Hi, Mom." Sam pushed her dad's phone against her ear and smiled. It smelled like the cologne he wore, her favorite.

"Hey, my girl. Looks like I probably won't make my flight home this afternoon. Not only is it pretty nasty here in New York, Dad says the flights at the Bill and Hillary Clinton Airport there are all delayed and some already canceled."

"I'm sorry, Mom."

"Me too. But at least you get a snow day, right?"

Sam grinned. "Yep."

Chewy barked at the kitchen door. Sam leaned and let the dog back in.

"Well, you have a good day. I'll keep you and Dad updated on my travel situation. I love you."

"Love you too, Mom. Bye." Sam tapped END CALL on the screen before handing the iPhone back to Dad.

"I talked with Captain York. I need to go into the office for a couple of hours, just to make sure everything's covered in the weather. Once officers show up, I'll be able to come back home." Dad poured coffee into his ginormous thermos. "Mrs. Willis is next door if you need anything."

"I'm good, Dad. Call me before you head home and I'll fix us grilled cheese sandwiches and soup for lunch."

"Deal." Dad grinned and kissed the top of her head.

"And, Dad?"

"Yeah, pumpkin?"

"If it's okay with Makayla's parents, do you think maybe you could pick her up on your way home for her to come over? Maybe spend the night since I bet they'll cancel school tomorrow?" She smiled wide and big.

"I'm pretty sure it'll be canceled," Dad chuckled. "It's fine with me if they say it's okay."

"Thanks."

"I'll call you when I'm leaving the precinct." Dad grabbed his keys from the wooden bowl in the foyer, then his footsteps echoed down the hall and into the garage.

Sam pulled out her phone again and dialed Makayla's cell.

"Snow day!" Makayla said as soon as she answered. "Isn't it beautiful? The news said we got about six inches total."

"That much? Wow."

"I know, right? Chloe's already done with breakfast so we can get into our snowsuits and get out there." Makayla giggled. "I think she thinks it's all going to melt soon."

"Six inches? Not hardly." Sam turned on the speaker so she could use both hands to get the boiling milk out of the microwave. "I bet they'll cancel school tomorrow too. No way this stuff is gonna be gone by then."

"Weather said we're not going to get over freezing, so I bet we will. We're also supposed to get some sleet and freezing rain later tonight."

That pretty much meant Mom wasn't going to make it back to Little Rock today. Probably not until later this weekend.

Sam brought the phone back up to her ear. "Dad had to go in to work this morning, but he's going to be heading back around lunchtime. He said it's okay if you come over, and you can spend the night if your parents say it's okay. He could pick you up on his way home."

"That'd be awesome! Let me ask Mom. Hang on."

While Sam waited, she stirred her hot chocolate. She pulled the can of whipped cream from the refrigerator and added it until it stood an inch higher than the cup. For good measure, she squirted some in her mouth straight from the can before putting it back in the fridge.

"I have a few chores I need to do first, but Mom said it's okay. I can come and spend the night."

"Woohoo! I'll text Dad and let him know. He said he would call before he left the station. We're gonna have so much fun."

"Let me go so I can play with Chloe real quick, then get my chores done. Oh, and pack a bag."

"Okay. I'll call you when Dad's on his way. Bye." Sam ended the call, then texted her dad to let him know he could pick up Makayla on his way home.

After eating a bowl of cereal and cleaning up the kitchen, Sam took a long hot shower, dressed, and then headed back to the kitchen where she put together a little basket of a couple of cans of soup, some of the chocolates left over from New Year's, and some packets of apple cider mix. She topped the basket with a ribbon, then put on her snow stuff and headed outside.

Cold air blasted around her. Despite her careful bundling up, a chill snaked down her spine. She trudged through the snow across the driveway to Mrs. Willis' yard. Stomping the snow from her boots, Sam rang the doorbell and waited for her neighbor to answer.

"Why, Sam! Dear, what are you doing out in this wintry weather?" Mrs. Willis opened the door and practically pulled Sam inside.

"Here. I brought this for you." Sam thrust the basket at her.

"For ... me?" Mrs. Willis smiled and took the basket. "This is lovely, Sam. Thank you."

"You're welcome." She started to feel very warm — almost suffocatingly so. Mrs. Willis sure had her heat turned up high. "Is there anything you need? I can shovel your walk if you need it done." She didn't really want to, but she was determined to love her neighbor.

"Shovel my walk? Whatever for? I don't plan on going anywhere."

"Do you need any food? Milk or eggs or bread?" Sam couldn't remember if they had extra, but if they didn't, she could text Dad and he'd pick something up on his way home.

"I'm good, dear. Thank you though." She waved toward her couch. "Would you like to come in and sit for a little visit?"

"I can't stay, Mrs. Willis." Sam found it hard to breathe in the stifling heat in just the few minutes she'd been inside. "I just wanted to check on you and bring you the basket."

"Well, it was very thoughtful of you. I'm fine. I have plenty of groceries, my butane tank was just filled last week, and I have my police scanner with batteries, so I'm all set." Mrs. Willis considered it part of her prayer ministry to pray for those involved in what came over the police scanner.

"Okay then. If you need anything, you just call us, okay?" Sam headed to the door.

"I will. And you too, dear. If you need anything."

Sam nodded, then stepped outside. The arctic air was welcome after being inside the stuffiness of Mrs. Willis' living room. She made her way back into the garage, then into the house.

Chewy met her at the door, hopping and prancing.

Sam laughed. "Okay. We'll go out back and play. Let me shut the garage door." She reached over to push the button, then went into the back yard with her dog. They played a rousing game of fetch until Sam felt her feet were freezing.

Back in the house, Sam dried Chewy off with an old beach towel, shoved her outwear into the dryer and turned it on, then set her boots on top of the dryer. She wanted everything dry and ready for more outdoor play once Makayla got there.

Her cell rang. Probably Dad. She checked the caller-ID. Not Dad. She answered the call. "Hi, Felicia." Sam headed toward her bedroom.

"I thought you were my friend." Felicia's voice sounded as hard as it had the first time Sam had heard her in the school office.

Sam froze. "I am. What's wrong?"

"If you're my friend, why did you tell why I was expelled from my last school?"

"I didn't." Sam's stomach turned.

"You didn't tell anyone? Not a single person?"

She'd told Makayla, but Mac wouldn't ever repeat that. "Why do you think I told someone?" Sam's heart skipped a beat.

"Well, there were only two people that I know of who knew. Mrs. Trees, who I doubt told any student, and you." Felicia made a snorting sound. "Shows I shouldn't trust my own judgment. I thought you were my friend."

"I am your friend, Felicia!"

"Were you just pretending to be my friend so you could get information from me to use? And what, were you scared to use your real name? Maybe little miss editor isn't as mean as I first thought. Maybe you're the mean one and she's just had enough."

Aubrey not mean? Not use her real name? This wasn't making any sense. "Felicia, I have no idea what you're talking about."

"Oh really?"

"Honestly, I haven't a clue." But she was tired of being accused of doing something she didn't do.

"Honestly ... that's rich, considering."

"Felicia, you're going to have to fill me in here because I have no idea what you're talking about." Sam slumped onto her bed.

"Have you seen the paper's blog this morning?"

A sinking feeling set in the pit of Sam's stomach. How could she have forgotten to check the newspaper's blog?

"No." She'd been so excited about school being canceled and Makayla getting to come over, then checking on Mrs. Willis that she hadn't even thought about the paper. What did that say about her as a reporter? She moved to her desk.

"You might want to check it out. If you didn't write it, and you didn't tell anyone else, then you tell me how that got posted up."

"I'll call you back." Sam set down her phone and began to read.

> The weather has closed the schools in PCSSD as well as the district office, but the offices of the *Senator Speak* are always open for business. After much discovery work, I've received further information regarding our report card virus problem.
>
> This editor has it on good authority that one of our transfer students was expelled from Pulaski Academy for attempted grade tampering. Sound familiar?
>
> … Sound Off, Senators, and leave a comment as to what you think should happen to this student. ~ Aubrey Damas, editor-in-chief, reporting

No wonder Felicia was furious. Sam would be too. The nerve of Aubrey! What was she up to? Sam swallowed hard. Where had Aubrey gotten the information?

Felicia said she'd only told Sam. Her records would have it listed, but who had access to those? Mrs. Trees? Mrs. Creegle? Some of the student office workers?

But how did Aubrey find out today? The school was closed. And no way would Aubrey have had this information before now and not used it. She was too much of a know-it-all to allow for that. No, she'd written the article and posted it as soon as she'd gotten the information about Felicia.

Especially since Aubrey didn't like Felicia. Then again, Aubrey didn't like hardly anyone except herself.

Sam checked the time of the post. Twenty-eight minutes ago.

What was going on here? Sam was determined to get to the bottom of it.

CHAPTER TWELVE

I have no idea where Aubrey got her information, Dad, so I can't be sure, but I'm pretty positive no one told her. The only people who know the reasons behind Felicia's expulsion are Felicia and the office, and I know for a fact that Felicia didn't tell her, and I'm pretty sure Mrs. Trees didn't tell her. I bet she stole the information somehow." Sam sat across the table from him, tearing apart her grilled cheese sandwich.

"You don't know that," Makayla gently admonished. She sat beside Sam, dipping her sandwich into the steaming bowl of tomato soup.

"No, I don't *know* that, but I can't imagine how else she'd get that information. I mean, school's closed. I seriously doubt Mrs. Trees called Aubrey to give her this information." Sam snorted and went to stirring her soup. She just couldn't concentrate with that article hovering over her head. "Even though she doesn't use Felicia's name, people have guessed. I imagine her mom is more than a little upset."

"And Felicia never told Aubrey?" Dad asked.

"Of course not. I emailed Mrs. Pape and told her the whole deal and asked her to pull down the post, but she hasn't responded. The only people who can remove a post are Mrs. Trees, Mrs. Pape, and Aubrey." Sam shoved a bite of her torn grilled cheese into her mouth. Even the warm, stringy cheddar didn't lift her spirits like it usually did.

Mrs. Pape probably wouldn't even check her email today. She was probably out playing in the snow with her little boy who'd turned three just before Christmas.

"Have you tried to call Aubrey and just ask her where she got her information?" Dad asked. "Maybe explain the situation and ask her to take down the article?"

Sam stared at him. She took a drink of sweet tea so she wouldn't choke on the sandwich that suddenly felt like a whole loaf of bread in the back of her throat.

Dad wiped his mouth with his napkin. "I know you two don't get along very well, but if you — "

"Get along well? Dad, she despises me. She goes out of her way to be mean to me."

"Are you sure you aren't blowing it out of proportion?" He slurped another spoonful of soup, raising just one of his eyebrows.

She turned to her bestie. "Mac, tell him."

Makayla nodded and swallowed her last bite. "She's not exaggerating, Mr. Sanderson. Aubrey does come at Sam pretty harsh most of the time."

Sam looked at her dad. "And before you ask, I don't know why she despises me. I can't think of a single thing I've done to her." She remembered her thoughts from the other day about Aubrey being hurt. She couldn't think of any time she'd hurt Aubrey. If she had, it wasn't intentional, and unless she knew about it, she couldn't apologize or make it right.

Although, to be honest, apologizing to Aubrey would probably choke her.

"If you want to know her source badly enough, I think you're going to have to just ask her." Dad took a drink of his sweet tea. The ice cubes rattled as he set the glass back on the table and stared at Sam with that look of his ... the one that meant you-should-just-do-as-I-suggest. "I can't think of any other way you'll find out."

"Not that she'll tell me. Or tell me the truth." It would be quite the bitter pill to swallow to call Aubrey and ask her for her source. She'd gloat, no doubt. Probably tell everybody how she scooped Sam on her own story and then Sam crawled to her to find out who her source was.

Sam shivered at the thought.

"Maybe Mrs. Pape will answer your email," Makayla offered.

"Maybe." Probably not. Sam sighed. "It's really irresponsible of Aubrey to have not gotten verification, either, which I doubt she even bothered to try and get. I mean, even though she didn't use Felicia's name, it's fairly obvious."

Dad and Makayla set down their spoons and stared at her.

"What?"

"Sam . . ." Dad threw her his *bulldog* look.

"What?" She glanced from her father to Makayla, annoyed.

His tone was softer, which was a little scary since it usually meant a reprimand was on the way. "Pumpkin, if you had been in Aubrey's shoes and gotten that information, and you weren't friends with Felicia, you probably would have written an article very similar to Aubrey's and posted it up."

Heat spread across the back of her neck and into her cheeks. "But I only use reliable sources." But her gut tightened in a sickening grip.

Makayla set her napkin in her empty bowl. "But Aubrey apparently did use a reliable source as well. The information is correct. You only know Felicia's side of it because Felicia told you."

Suddenly, Sam didn't feel very well. Dad and Makayla were right. She would've done the same thing as Aubrey. She was only upset right now because it hurt a friend of hers.

CHAPTER TWELVE

Had any of her stories ever hurt someone who was innocent?

Sam didn't want that. Maybe she wasn't cut out to be a reporter after all if it meant hurting others. Hurting innocent people sure wasn't loving neighbors. Maybe she should totally rethink her whole career plan.

Dad polished off the last bite of his sandwich. "On a more positive note, Mom's made it to DFW airport and thinks she can get on a standby flight. Here's hoping she can make it here tonight," he said, smiling.

"What if she can't? She'll just have to sleep at an airport terminal?" Sam shivered. That would just be nasty. Every airport she'd been to, even the really nice ones, weren't places she'd like to be stranded.

Dad chuckled. "If she can't make the last flight out, she'll just stay at one of the Hyatt hotels on airport property. Don't worry, she won't sleep on one of those germy couches."

"Good, cuz those things are gross." Sam smiled, then got serious. "Dad, has the cyber unit done anything on the case? Off the record."

He smiled. "Off the record, not that I know of. Like I told you, they're still trying to sort through all the problems with the stolen credit and debit card information over the holidays."

Sam glanced at Makayla, then back at her dad. Makayla elbowed her and gave a little shake of her head.

"What's going on, girls?" Dad asked.

Makayla frowned and shot Sam a look that clearly said to let the matter drop.

But Sam couldn't let it go. "Well, there's a way we might be able to get you some information that might help you identify who's behind the virus."

"Really?" Dad's eyes widened as his brows shot up. "Please share."

Sam briefly filled him in on the basics of hers and Makayla's conversation yesterday.

"So virus creators usually have a specific method in the way they write their virus code?" he asked, looking straight at Makayla.

She nodded. "More or less, yes. There are certain little strands that really don't affect the virus or program, but are just a specific preference by the code writer. Like, specific colors for the lines of code or something like that. It's usually identifiable because it's usually used more than once. Once that snippet of code is identified, it can be run against a database of known virus creators or whatever the police's cyber unit has."

Dad nodded, clearly impressed. "You sure know a lot about this, Makayla."

She grinned. "I'm not interested in creating havoc viruses, Mr. Sanderson, but I'm learning a lot from the computer research demographic group I'm in. We have a lot of people who do create viruses, but only to learn how to disable them. Just like how I'm in the hackers group, where we deliberately try to hack into a system just to see if we can. It's all pretty cool." She nodded toward Sam. "It's not too late to submit an application to join the group."

"Uh, no thanks. Told you, it's not where my interests are." Sam grabbed hers, Dad's, and Makayla's plates and took them into the kitchen. "Dad, Mac can go in and poke around and see if she can find one of those identifier codes. If she does, you could turn that over to the cyber unit and help them get a head start."

"I can't promise I'll be able to find anything," Makayla protested.

Sam rolled her eyes at her father as she went back to the table to collect the glasses. "If it's there, she'll find it. And she can look around and see if there's a self-destruct installed."

"Maybe. I might not be able to identify it even if I see it."

"Stop being all modest, Mac. Dad knows you're a ninja computer genius."

Makayla blushed.

Dad put up his hand to stop her. "Before you get too carried away, let me think about it. I want to make a couple of calls to one of our cyber unit guys first."

"Sure, Mr. Sanderson, we understand." Mac cut her eyes to Sam and narrowed them to little slits. No mistaking the warning to Sam.

Sam ran over and hugged her dad. "Thanks for even considering it!" She grabbed Makayla's hand. "Come on, let's go make some snow angels." She led her down the hall to her room, Chewy following.

"I can't believe you just asked your dad like that." Makayla stepped out of Sam's bathroom a few minutes later and began wrapping her head with a scarf.

"What else was I supposed to do? You won't go poking without permission, and now, with Aubrey's article up, I'm backed against a wall."

"You got game, girl." Makayla pulled her ski cap over the scarf.

Sam finished braiding her hair and slipped on her hat. "I've got to do something, Mac. It's not fair for Aubrey to write such an article about Felicia."

"At least she didn't use Felicia's name."

"Yeah, but that didn't help much." She shook her head. "Felicia's mom was already wary of it all, and now this." Sam wrapped her scarf around her neck and tucked the ends into her sweatshirt. "Aubrey Damas is just plain mean."

"Sam, that's not fair. She was just reporting, just like you would've done and you know it."

Sam frowned. "I would not have done such a thing to Felicia."

"Not to someone you know, of course not, but Aubrey doesn't really know Felicia at all, does she?" Makayla held up her hands. "Don't get mad at me. I'm not saying you do anything mean or wrong, but sometimes telling the truth doesn't tell the whole story. That's the case here."

"Hmmm," Sam said, but her mind raced. Maybe she should be a little more sensitive when she wrote her own articles. She'd never be able to *not* tell the truth, but maybe she could work a little harder to dig deeper into the truth.

Makayla put on her gloves and coat. "Come on, let's go out and play for a while and forget all about viruses, grade tampering, and Aubrey Damas."

Chewy, hearing the words *out* and *play*, started wagging and jumping. Sam laughed and rubbed between the dog's ears. "Come on, you can come with us this time."

An hour later, they stumbled back into the house, feet frozen, dripping wet, but laughing. Dad met them at the door. "Get out of those wet clothes and come have some hot cocoa."

"That's what I'm talking about," Sam said. In less than fifteen minutes, they were curled up on the sofa with steaming cups of hot chocolate with whipped cream. Dad had even sprinkled mini chocolate chips on top of the whipped cream.

Totally yummy.

The fire Dad had built roared, popping and hissing as he added another log. Chewy lay on the rug in front of the fire. Sam felt warm and toasty, inside and out. If only Mom were home, then it would be perfect.

And if she could fix things for Felicia.

"Sam, I'm going to need a favor." Dad didn't smile. His hands rested on his knees.

She couldn't think of a single time he'd come to her asking for a favor. She set her mug on the coffee table. "Sure, Dad." Unless, of course, he asked her to give up reporting. That would never happen, but she doubted he'd ever ask her to do that. "If I can."

"I need you to call Aubrey and see if you can find out where she got her information."

The hot chocolate and whipped cream felt like it curdled on Sam's stomach. "Why?" How could he ask her to do this? She'd told him how much of a jerk Aubrey was.

"Off the record?" Dad looked from Sam to Makayla. Both of them nodded.

Dad ran a hand through his salt and pepper hair, though it was more salt than pepper these days. "My captain called me asking if you had anything to do with what Aubrey printed. It seems his son also transferred in from Pulaski Academy. He's concerned that some people might think the person Aubrey's referring to in her article is his son."

Sam's eyes widened. "Doug was expelled from PA?"

"No, he wasn't expelled." Dad leaned forward, on the edge of the chair. "This is totally off the record, right?"

She nodded. Beside her, Makayla nodded as well.

"Doug didn't get expelled, but he was about to flunk out. Captain transferred him out to save the embarrassment."

"Flunk out?" Sam twisted to look at her best friend. "Didn't you say Doug was even better than you in computer science?"

Makayla nodded. "Mr. Sanderson, Doug's probably the smartest person I've seen in programming and such. There's no way he'd flunk out. He probably knows more than most high school kids."

"That's just in one class, girls. He might have been flunking in other subjects."

Sam shrugged. "I guess so. But we all know Aubrey was referring to Felicia in the article, so why does your boss need to know Aubrey's source? The article's already published, so what good is it to him to know who told Aubrey?" Sure, she wanted to know, but she didn't like the captain's assumption that he should have the right to know who a source was.

Wanting to be a hard-core journalist, Sam was very sensitive about protecting sources. There were measures in place to protect all journalists, even those in middle school, against pressure to force them to reveal their sources. That Captain York seemed to want to work around them left a real sour taste in Sam's mouth.

"He could, but he's asking me if you were involved, Sam. He knows you and Doug aren't exactly chummy, but he did imply that you might have something to do with Aubrey's evasive article."

"Are you kidding me? Seriously?" Sam jumped to her

feet, startling Chewy, who darted away. "As if I would give Aubrey any type of credit for something I uncovered!" Sam paced the span of the living room.

"I know that. I'm just asking if you'll call Aubrey. If you get a name, I can assure Captain York that you passed along no such information about his son."

"I didn't even know until you told me."

"I understand."

She made another lap around the living room. *Love my neighbor.* Yeah, that's real helpful right now. What about protecting her sources? What about the shield law?

"Dad, I know what you're saying, but your boss is basically using me to get around the shield law where Aubrey's concerned." Sam couldn't believe that she was defending Aubrey. She wasn't, really. She was defending the rights of journalists to protect their sources.

"Um, what's the shield law?" Makayla asked.

Sam pulled it up on her cell phone and read aloud, "Any editor, reporter, or other writer for any newspaper, periodical, or radio station is protected from revealing his or her sources unless the party seeking disclosure can show that the article was written in bad faith, with malice, and not in the interest of the public welfare."

"So," Makayla said as she wrinkled her nose, "Aubrey, acting as the school editor, doesn't have to reveal who told her about Felicia because the article she wrote wasn't written in bad faith or with malice?"

"Well, I think Aubrey wrote with malice because she hates Felicia, but that can't be proven." Sam looked at her father.

"Don't you want to know who told Aubrey?" Makayla asked.

"I do, but I don't want to get the name and then turn it over to Captain York. That would be wrong, like I was supporting forcing someone to reveal their sources. I just feel wrong about it."

"What's your gut telling you?" Dad asked.

That was the problem. She was conflicted. On one hand, she wanted to help Felicia. On the other, she wanted to support reporters' rights to protect their sources. Man, she wished Mom was home. What to do?

Love your neighbor as yourself. Didn't that mean treating your neighbor as you want to be treated?

If she was Felicia, she'd want to know who told about her past. The only way Sam could find out who told was to ask Aubrey. Not that she expected Aubrey to tell her. But Dad wasn't asking her to dig, he was simply asking her to ask Aubrey. If Aubrey told her, well, then she'd have to make a decision of whether or not they should tell Captain York.

"Okay. Fine." She pulled out her iPhone and scrolled to her contacts. All the newspaper staff had each other's contact information. Mrs. Pape had insisted. "Here goes nothing." She tapped the phone and it connected.

Brrring!

Sam went back to her pacing. Maybe Aubrey was outside and couldn't hear her phone.

Brrring!

Maybe Aubrey forgot to turn up the ringer on her phone.

Brrring!

More likely, Aubrey was torturing someone so she had the phone on silent.

Brr — "What do you want, Samantha Sanderson?" Even on a day off, Aubrey sounded as grumpy and ill-tempered as usual.

"Hi, Aubrey. Enjoying your snow day?"

"I was until you called. What do you want?"

Sam put her finger to her lips for her dad and Makayla to see, then set her phone on the coffee table and turned on the speaker. "I read your article up on the blog."

Aubrey laughed, but it wasn't in a funny sort of way. "So that's why you're calling. Jealous because I found out something you didn't?"

"I already knew, Aubrey. I actually know the whole story, and I know the person you were referring to didn't set a virus loose in our school's system."

"Sure you knew. That's why *you* wrote the article instead of me, right?" Aubrey laughed in that humorless way of hers again. "Look, Samantha, just accept it. I'm a better reporter than you, and I have better sources."

Sam gritted her teeth and fisted then unfisted her hands. "Yeah, who is your source? Who told you about Felicia, Aubrey?"

"Oh, so you know who it is. I'm impressed. I thought you wouldn't have guessed."

"I told you I knew. Felicia told me." Sam concentrated on not letting anger seep into her voice. "Who told you?"

"Wouldn't you like to know? And if Felicia told you, why didn't you use it for an article, huh?" Aubrey cackled. "You're lying, Samantha Sanderson, because now everybody knows that I'm a better reporter than you are."

"Aubrey, how did you find out?"

"Wouldn't you like to know? I'm not telling you. Maybe you should use the *reporter instincts* your mommy taught you to figure it out. I'm done wasting my time on you."

The call disconnected.

Sam was so mad, she trembled.

"Well, I guess I was wrong when I thought you might be exaggerating how Aubrey treats you." Dad even looked upset.

"See? I told you she was horrid. Lana calls her the she-beast."

"She's really like that all the time, Mr. Sanderson," Makayla said.

Dad shook his head. "I guess I'd forgotten how vicious girls can be."

"Yeah." Sam pocketed her phone. "Sorry she wouldn't give me a name, but I didn't figure she would. She's mean like that."

"Thanks for trying." Dad stood, but didn't walk away. His tone told her he was in pure dad-mode now. "About what you asked permission for ..."

Sam's heart pounded hard against her ribs. "Yeah?" *Please say yes. Please say yes.*

His cell rang. He checked the caller-ID, held up a finger to the girls, and answered the call. "Hi, honey."

"Mom," Sam mouthed to Makayla.

"No kidding. I kinda figured that out by the *honey*," Makayla whispered.

"That's great. Okay. Text me when you land. I'll head to the airport then to get you. Love you." Dad slipped his phone back into his pocket. "Mom's gotten on one of the standby flights. They should start boarding within thirty minutes."

"That's great." Sam was glad Mom would be home tonight, but right now ... "So, you were saying ... ?"

"Yes, Miss One-track Mind." He grinned at Sam. "I talked with a friend of mine in the cyber unit." Sam's dad looked at Makayla. "He said he sure would appreciate it if you would look into the system to see if you can find out anything on the virus."

Score! "Yes!" Sam all but danced around the living room. Chewy, who had returned to the rug in from the fireplace, watched her with wary eyes.

"If you're willing, of course," Dad said, addressing Makayla. "If you aren't comfortable with doing it, that's okay. I know how pushy she can be sometimes." He nodded at Sam and threw Mac an apologetic look.

"Hey." Sam put her hands on her hips. "I just called the she-beast because you asked, so let's not talk about being pushy."

Dad laughed, reaching out to pull Sam in for a hug. "Touché, pumpkin." He turned back to Makayla. "It's totally up to you."

"I-I think I'd like to help, if I can."

Sam grinned. "Awesome. I'll bring my MacBook in here."

Dad pointed at the computer on the desk in the corner of the living room. "Why can't you use that one?"

Sam and Makayla both laughed.

"Dad, that thing's so out of date. Besides, she needs to use a Mac so that there's no chance that the virus could infect our computer. I'll grab my MacBook real quick." She darted to her room, snatched up her laptop, and returned to the living room.

Sam set up the laptop on the coffee table, then stood and motioned to Makayla to sit the couch. "It's all ready for you, milady."

Sam hovered over her bestie and crossed her fingers. This had to work. It just had to.

CHAPTER THIRTEEN

I 'll need to access the system remotely. Give me a second." Makayla's fingers flew over the laptop's keys.

Dad sat back in his recliner while Sam inched to the edge of the couch. Chewy had curled back up on the rug and closed her eyes. Sam clasped her hands in her lap so she wouldn't be tempted to tap her finger against the table. She didn't want to do anything to distract Makayla from her probing.

"Okay, I'm connecting. Keep your fingers crossed that they didn't put up a new security firewall before Christmas break."

"Doubtful, otherwise the virus probably wouldn't have infected the system," Sam said as she bounced her knee.

"Not necessarily." Makayla leaned closer to the monitor. "Doesn't matter. I'm in." She let out a slow breath. "Now let's see if I can get into the grading system program." Her fingers moved fast over the keys as she kept her eyes narrowed. Squinting.

Sam didn't want to make a sound. She didn't even swallow.

"That didn't work. Let's try this." Makayla typed some more.

Dad met Sam's stare, the question of what Makayla was trying now plain in his eyes. Sam shrugged. She didn't have a clue, but had total faith in her best friend.

"Okay, that didn't work. Hmm." Makayla popped her lips. Again. And again. "How about this way?" She typed again. A pause. Then she growled. "I'm starting to take this personal."

Only the *tap-tap-tap* of the keys sounded in the living room.

"If you can't get in, that's okay," Dad offered.

Makayla's eyes lit up. "It's okay, Mr. Sanderson. I think I figured it out."

Sam rocked beside Makayla. *Please, please, please let her get in.*

Makayla did an air punch. "Got it. Okay, now let's see if I can get into the code itself. Let me see." Makayla went from typing, to tapping her chin, then back to typing.

Sam and her dad remained silent.

"Ah, there you are. I found it." Makayla smiled and her eyes went wide. She got as jazzed about this computer stuff as Sam got in finding a lead on an article. "I'm going to look at the code now."

"Told you," Sam mouthed to her dad. He grinned back at her.

"Interesting." Makayla actually smiled at the computer screen.

"What?" Sam asked.

"There is a self-destruct file embedded, but it isn't set to activate when the system attempts a restart from backup."

Sam's dad looked at her. She shrugged. "Oh, really?" she asked Makayla, because she didn't know what else to say.

"Yeah. It's here, but ..." She made a few more keystrokes. "It's set to self-destruct if the program starts a backup. That's really weird."

"Why is that?" Dad asked. "What's the difference?"

"A restart from backup is just that, restarting the whole system from a backup. A program backup is when someone tries to copy the data of a particular program." Makayla lifted her gaze from the computer. "Well, if I'm reading this right, and of course, I might be wrong. I could be wrong. I probably am. You should probably get someone else — "

"Mac!" Sam loved her bestie dearly, but sometimes ...

"Okay." Makayla cleared her throat and continued. "If what I think is right, then when this particular program is set to backup, the virus will self-destruct and remove itself from the system."

"And the whole issue will be gone?" Sam asked.

Makayla nodded. "As if it wasn't ever on the system."

"So why hasn't it uninstalled itself? Don't the servers back up every night?" Sam asked.

"The servers do, with the basic data bits of information, but the programs have to be set to back up independently. As soon as the district's IT team figured out there was a virus, they probably cut off the program from the regular system so as to not infect the rest of the system. A smart security measure. When they cut this program off, the backups were halted."

"I'm not sure I understand." Dad ran his fingers through his hair again.

Makayla smiled. "Whoever did this didn't intend for there to be permanent damage to the program or the system."

"I see. I think." Dad's brow puckered.

Makayla made a clucking sound with her tongue.

"What is it?" Dad asked.

"I also found something else interesting," Makayla said.

"What?" Sam asked.

"This virus was actually introduced into the system before we went on Christmas break, before the grades would be put in the program." Makayla grinned over the monitor.

"What? Are you sure?"

Makayla nodded. "Positive. It was introduced right

about the time school dismissed on the last Friday before break."

"You can tell that by looking at the code?" Sam asked.

She nodded again. "Yep, it's pretty easy once you know what you're looking for. Want me to show you?"

Dad cleared his throat and nodded at the computer. "Did you find any of those identifiers you were talking about that could help us figure out who is responsible?"

"Oh. I haven't looked yet." She put her fingers on the keyboard, then lifted them again. "Sam, do you have a sixteen gig jump drive?"

"Sure. You need it?"

"Please. I'm going to try and copy the virus' code onto a drive so we have a copy of the full virus code. This is a cool one, and should be studied. Analyzing viruses is the best way to learn how to create defenses against them."

"I'll get it." Sam ran to her room and snagged a USB stick from the middle drawer of her desk. She didn't know if she'd call any computer virus cool, but to each his own, she supposed. She returned and handed it to Makayla.

"Thanks." Makayla stuck the drive in the USB port, typed for a few seconds, then sat straight. "There, it's copying to the drive." She let out a little sigh. "I was worried it might not copy, but there it is. It's finished. All done." She ejected the drive and removed the stick, then her eyes went wide. "Oh, no."

"Oh, no, what?" Sam and her dad asked in unison.

"No, no, no!" Makayla pounded the keys.

"What?" Sam asked. "What's wrong?"

"It's going."

"What?" Sam's father asked. "What's going?"

"The virus. It's uninstalling itself." She typed frantically. "Stop." Makayla hit the keys harder. "Please, no. Come on. Quit." She slumped back against the couch.

Tears welled in her eyes and she wore the most disappointed expression.

"What?" Sam asked.

"It's gone."

"Gone? What do you mean, gone?"

"Just what I said. Gone. It's uninstalled. Poof."

Sam knew Makayla was going to start crying any minute now. It wasn't going to be pretty.

"Wait a minute," Dad intervened. "Are you telling me the virus is out of the program and off the server?"

Makayla nodded. "I'm so sorry, Mr. Sanderson. I guess it had another self-destruct file that would be activated if the virus was copied. I didn't see it, so I didn't realize it would uninstall itself when I ejected the copy."

"The virus is off the system, and you're ... apologizing?" He looked like he knew something Sam and Makayla didn't.

"Oh my goodness, Makayla. No, this is great. You just removed a virus that has the entire school in a holding pattern, has your principal in a snit, has kept the district's IT team guessing, and you're apologizing? No need." His voice was reassuring and confident.

Sam started laughing. "That is kinda funny, Mac. We've been chasing our tails to figure out how to get rid of the virus without causing more damage, and you did just it."

Makayla hesitated a moment, then began laughing too. "Okay, y'all got me. It's just when I saw the uninstaller eating all the code, I panicked. I don't know why."

"How you managed to do this and the IT team didn't is a little confusing," Dad said.

"Told you she had ninja computer skills," Sam said, grinning at her best friend.

"It's not that," Makayla said with a shake of her head. "IT has processes and procedures they have to follow. I don't." She grinned. "Especially when I panic."

Sam laughed again, and Dad did as well.

Chewy, not sure what was going on but sensing something, sat up, her ears perked and alert.

"I wonder if the eschoolplus information is correct." Sam pulled the laptop to her and logged on. It took a little longer than usual, but when she went to REPORT CARDS, her grades were correct: two Bs and the rest As. "Looks like it's good here."

"Well done, Makayla." Dad beamed.

A few moments passed before Sam could think clearly. "I guess we need to let Mrs. Trees and the district know, huh?"

SAMANTHA SANDERSON OFF THE RECORD

Dad stood and pulled out his cell. "I'll notify the captain, but since school and district offices are closed, I doubt he can get in touch with anybody about this. Although, he might have your principal's home phone number. She's been all about solving this mystery. Then I need to head to the airport to pick up Mom. Travel will be really slow with the weather." He moved into the kitchen, iPhone to his ear.

Sam turned the laptop and opened a blank blog document. The tapping sounded as she typed.

"What are you doing?" Makayla whispered so as to not interrupt Sam's dad on the phone.

"I'm writing an article and getting it posted up."

Makayla glanced at Sam's dad's back as he walked in the kitchen. "Is that okay with your dad? I mean, will he let you?"

"I don't know, and I'm not asking." Sam's fingers typed as fast as her mind organized the article, which was surprisingly fast.

> ... **That's right, Senators, the virus has been removed from the system with no damage left. So during this snow day, if you want to know what your grades really are, check your *e*schoolplus account. Sound Off, Senators, and leave a comment of how you're spending your snow day. ~ Sam Sanderson, reporting**

Her father hung up his phone just as Sam pressed the SEND button.

"Did you get in touch with anybody?" she asked as he rejoined them. Maybe she could distract him so he wouldn't ask her about what she was doing.

"I talked to Captain York and told him. He's going to try and reach Mrs. Trees at home." He nodded toward the computer. "What's going on?"

"Hey, is that sleet I hear hitting the window?" Sam stood and moved to the window and peeked through the blinds. "It is. Look. It's coming down pretty hard. Guess you need to get outta here so you don't keep Mom waiting at the airport." She pulled the cord to open the wood blinds.

Dad joined her at the window. "Looks like it's been sleeting for some time. Good thing I put the snow chains on my tires this morning. I'm sure the airport's a mess with all the delayed and canceled flights. But I don't need to leave yet. Her plane hasn't landed." He tapped the glass, pointing at the cedar trees in the Hardens' yard across the street. "Look at the trees leaning over from the weight of the ice."

"I think they're beautiful," Makayla breathed as she joined them. "Everything looks so sharp and clear."

"And deadly. Well, it can be." Sam's dad pointed at her. "Now, what were you two up to while I was on the phone?" He stepped into the foyer and lifted his coat from the hook.

"Nothing." Sam stretched with her arms high above her head, then headed to stand in front of the fireplace.

She sat on the hearth and stroked Chewy's head. "At least Makayla was able to copy the virus' code. I'm sure the cyber unit will want to analyze it to figure out who did it. They're lucky you were smart enough to make a copy, Mac." Sam smiled.

"Can I have a copy, Mr. Sanderson?" Makayla asked Sam's dad. "I mean, after the cyber unit techs are done with it? I think my group could learn from it. That's part of what our group does: learns how to break through virus code to learn how to disable them."

"She can have a copy. Right, Dad?"

"I don't know, Sam," he said.

"Why not? It's not like she's going to set it loose somewhere. Her group is government funded, so it's not like it's just some group of computer nerds out there acting on their own." She glanced at her bestie. "No offense."

"None taken."

Dad shook his head. "I don't think so. Not right now. Not until the case is closed."

Sam frowned. "We wouldn't have it at all if she hadn't copied it in the first place. What's the harm in making a copy of a copy?"

"I'll make sure you get a copy when the case is closed and we're done with the copy." Dad's cell phone rang. He pulled it out and headed into the kitchen to take the call.

Sam ran to her room and grabbed another jump drive, then ran back to the living room. She put both jump drives into the computer and began copying the virus.

"What are you doing?" Makayla hissed.

"Just making sure you get a copy. Gotta hurry. That might be Mom."

"Your dad said he'd get a copy back to me."

"Unless the cyber unit messes it up." The transfer was done. Sam ejected both drives and stuck one in her pocket.

"Your dad is going to flip," Makayla whispered.

"He'll never know. You aren't going to do anything bad with it." Sam shrugged. "Besides, you never know if we might need it."

"For what, pray tell?"

Dad returned to the living room. "That was my captain. He got in touch with Mrs. Trees and gave her the good news."

"Oh. That's good, right?" Sam asked, but Dad didn't look like it was good news.

"Sam, did you post up an article that the virus had been removed and everything was all clear?"

Her tongue felt four sizes too big for her mouth. She nodded slowly.

Dad sighed. "Why would you do that?"

"Because it's been my story. The virus being gone is news, Dad."

"You should have asked me before you posted it." He sounded very weary all of the sudden.

"Why? It's my story. This is news. Good news for a change."

"You wanted to prove Aubrey wrong. That she wasn't as good of a reporter and that you could get inside information." Dad shook his head and let out a very heavy sigh.

Sam chewed her lip and looked at the floor as her chest tightened.

"Makayla, could you look at the code on that drive and see if you can see any of those identifiers, please?"

"Sure, Mr. Sanderson." Makayla sat back down on the couch and popped the jump drive back in.

"What's going on, Dad?" Sam asked.

"My captain wants to know how we removed the virus. I had to explain that I asked you girls to look into the code. He's finding it hard to believe that a middle schooler, no matter how smart, could do what the district's IT team couldn't: isolate the virus and uninstall it without damaging the system unless they were involved in the creation of the virus to begin with. And the timing ... he mentioned that it seemed like perfect timing for you to be able to write an article for it so quickly."

"He thinks we created the virus so we were able to remove it? And that we timed it so I could scoop Aubrey? That's just ridiculous," Sam said, starting to pace again. Although, from Dad's point of view, he could probably understand Captain York's way of thinking.

Dad stared at Makayla, his face tense.

"Oh." Mac swallowed. "He doesn't think *we* did anything. He thinks *I* did, doesn't he, Mr. Sanderson?"

"I'm sorry, Makayla," Dad said. "Apparently Doug told his father that you were the only person he knew that was better with computer programs than he is."

Oh no. Makayla's mother was going to freak out big time if this became a big deal.

"I'm hoping you can find one of those identifiers you were telling me about so I can turn it over to the cyber unit. I'll put a rush on it so they can try and trace it back to the person who actually created the virus."

Makayla nodded. She hunched over the computer monitor and began scrolling.

Sam's mouth went dry as her heart pounded. "I'm so sorry. If I'd have known my story would stir up your boss and cause him to suspect Makayla, I never would have posted it." She never wanted Dad to get in trouble because of something she'd done, but she had. She felt awful and wanted desperately to make it right.

"I know, pumpkin, but this is a prime example of why I'm always telling you to not act rashly." He slipped his arms into his coat sleeves and pulled out a cap from the pocket. "I've got to go get your mother. Mrs. Willis is next door if you need anything."

Sam stared at her dad's retreating back, feeling lower than low. "I'm sorry, Mac." Sam dropped down on the couch beside her best friend.

"It's okay, Sam. I wasn't involved in designing the virus, so I have nothing to worry about, right?" But she didn't look so sure.

Sam felt horrible. Worse than horrible. Horrid on top of horrible. "What can I do to help?"

Makayla never took her eyes off the monitor or her fingers from the keyboard. "Get me a piece of paper and a pen, please."

"You found something?" Sam's dad asked as he retrieved his keys from the wooden bowl on the table in the entryway. He moved to stand beside Makayla and read over her shoulder.

"I think I found an identifier."

Sam grabbed a notepad from the desk and a pen that she handed to her best friend. Makayla scribbled a line of numbers and letters onto the paper.

"That's an identifier?" Sam's father asked.

"I think so. It's a font specification, including size and color. It keeps popping up in the coding."

"That's good, right?" Sam asked.

"If it's truly an identifier, yes. And if the police can trace it as a creator's MO, even better." Makayla ejected the drive. "That's all I could find." She pulled the drive from the computer.

The house lights went off. Chewy barked and growled.

"Mac, what did you do now?" Sam asked.

CHAPTER FOURTEEN

M e? I didn't do anything." Makayla's voice warbled. Dad's cell dinged. He stared at the message, then frowned. "I need to make a quick phone call." He headed into the kitchen.

Sam laughed and nudged Makayla. "I'm teasing you, girl. The electricity just went out." She pulled out her cell. Using the electric company's texting system, she reported the outage, then got an immediate confirmation of her report. "In fifteen minutes, I can request a status update of when they estimate power will be restored." She set the phone on the coffee table and sat beside Makayla.

Chewy danced around the living room, still growling.

"Sit, Chewy," Sam commanded. The dog lay down on the rug, staring up at Sam with her big, brown eyes.

Dad stepped back into the living room. His face seemed pale, even in the dimmed lights.

Sam stood. "Dad, what's wrong?"

He didn't say anything.

Dad's silence unnerved her. "If this is about your captain, I'll be happy to explain it to him myself," Sam said. "I'll talk to Doug and see if he can talk to his dad. I can try and get Mrs. Pape to pull my blog down. Just tell me what you want me to do." Sam had never seen Dad look so serious.

"It's not that. Sit down."

As she sat down slowly on the couch beside Makayla, Sam's heart raced. "Dad, you're scaring me."

"I just spoke with an airport representative."

Sam swallowed against a dry mouth. Her stomach was in knots. An airport representative? What was wrong?

"The news is that your mom's plane had an accident during landing. It hit ice on the runway and slid into a bunker."

Nonononono! Sam sucked in air.

Makayla reached over and grabbed Sam's hand and squeezed it.

"I have to go to the airport. I don't know any more than there was the accident. I'm going to get Mrs. Willis to come stay with you two."

Sam jumped to her feet, pulling Makayla up as well. "Dad, I want to come with you. Is Mom okay? Is she hurt?" *Is she alive? No, she had to be alive. She had to be okay. She was **Mom**.*

"I don't know, and you need to stay here. You can't come with me." He put his hands on her shoulders and stared down into her eyes. "Please, Sam, don't argue about this with me. I have to go."

Sam opened her mouth, but Makayla squeezed her hand harder.

"I'll call you as soon as I know something." He gave Sam a quick hug. "I'm going to get Mrs. Willis." He disappeared down the hall. Chewy followed, her nails tapping on the floor. The door to the garage slammed. Chewy returned to the living room, whining as if she understood something very bad had happened.

"Mac?" Sam turned to her, unwanted tears blurring her vision. She didn't even care that she was about to cry. She was so scared. She'd never been so scared before.

Makayla hugged her. "It's going to be okay. I started praying as soon as your dad told us."

"It's Mom."

"I know." Makayla helped her back to the couch. "Let's pray together, okay?"

Sam nodded, but her nose had started running along with the tears. She bowed her head.

"Dear God, we ask You to keep Sam's mother safe.

We know You love her so much, and Sam and her dad. We pray You'll watch over Sam's dad as he drives on the slippery streets to get to the airport. We ask that You keep everyone safe, God. And I ask that You fill Sam with peace and comfort, knowing You're keeping her parents safe. In Jesus' name we pray, Amen."

Sam sniffed. "Thanks." And while she was still really scared, she didn't feel as panicky as she had a few minutes ago. She still felt sick to her stomach though.

Chewy leaned against Sam's leg and whined. Sam reached down and petted her, letting the dog's warm fur comfort her.

The door leading in from the garage door opened. Chewy barked and took off down the hall.

"Sam?" Mrs. Willis' voice rang down the hall. "Hi, Chewy. It's just me."

"We're in here," Makayla answered.

Mrs. Willis rounded the corner, Chewy right beside her. "Oh, Sam, sweetheart." She held open her arms.

Sam rushed into them and accepted the hug.

"It's going to be okay, dear. I was listening to my police scanner and heard about it, not knowing your momma was on that plane. I'd already started praying for the people as soon as it came over the scanner."

"We've prayed too," Makayla added.

"Hello, Makayla, dear. So nice that you're here with Sam." Mrs. Willis made her way to sit in Dad's recliner, careful to step around Chewy who couldn't seem to sit still. "Your father said he'd call as soon as he knew anything."

Sam hated waiting. She began pacing. The only sound thumping in her ears was the sound of her footfalls. Earlier, the popping from the fireplace had been such a comforting sound. Now, it mocked her with the silence. "Mrs. Willis, can we listen to your scanner?"

"That's probably not a good idea, dear."

Yeah, because if something went seriously wrong... no, she couldn't think like that. But she couldn't stand not knowing either. "It'd make me feel a whole lot better. Please?"

"I suppose I could go get it." The older lady made rocking motions as if to propel herself out of the recliner.

"No. I'll get it." Sam headed to the laundry room and slipped on her winter wear.

"It's unlocked, and you know where the scanner is."

"I'll be right back." Sam let Chewy out into the backyard, then rushed herself into the bitter cold. Sleet pelted her, but she welcomed the beating. Her imagination wouldn't stop replaying every single plane crash scene she'd ever seen on the news or in a movie, which was illogical, since Dad hadn't said there'd been a crash at all. A slick landing, that's what he'd said. Slid into a bunker. But her mind kept seeing a fiery mess that made her heart stop.

God, please keep Mom safe.

Sam shook her head to clear her thoughts as she let herself into Mrs. Willis' house. In just the short time they'd been without power, her neighbor's normally overly warm and stuffy house had taken on a chill. She grabbed the police scanner from the kitchen table where Mrs. Willis always kept it, then headed back out into the cold and sleet. As she rounded Mrs. Willis's carport, she heard a faint little sound.

Sam stopped and listened carefully. Sleet pinged against metal and vinyl siding. Maybe she'd imagined hearing something. Her boots crunched on the snow and ice.

Rahr.

What *was* that? It sounded so feeble. An animal? Out here in this nasty weather? Maybe she was just imagining things.

Rowr.

Closer, but sounding fainter. A cat? Sam set the police scanner inside her open garage, then stepped back into the yard. She held her breath to listen better.

Meow. Meow.

There, from the little side swatch of lawn between her house and Mrs. Willis'. Sam walked toward the sound. "Here, kitty kitty."

Chewy barked from the fenced back yard. "Shh, Chewy," Sam said, stopping to listen for sounds of the cat.

Meow.

From the right. Sam took three more steps and then she saw it, barely. It was a little white kitten, so white that it blended with the snow. Its little pink nose and ears were soaked. "Shh, it's okay." She slowly bent down to pick up the kitten.

Meow.

The poor little thing was soaking wet and shivering. It couldn't be more than a month old and its fur wasn't very thick. Not enough to keep it warm.

Chewy started barking again.

"Shh, Chewy. Be quiet." Sam unzipped her coat and snuggled the kitten next to her chest. She zipped her coat again, then rushed to the garage. She grabbed the scanner, stomped her feet, then went inside. The kitten purred against her.

"Makayla!"

"What? What is it?" Makayla stepped into the laundry room.

Sam set the scanner on top of the dryer. "Look what I found outside." She unzipped her coat and pulled out the kitten, who immediately began crying.

"Oh my goodness. You poor thing." Makayla took the soaked kitten and tucked it under her chin. "Where'd you find it?"

"Hovering next to Mrs. Willis' house." Sam hung her coat on the hook and threw her gloves, scarf, and cap into the dryer. She pulled off her boots, then pulled off a beach towel from the shelf over the washer and dryer.

She gently took the kitten from Makayla and wrapped it in the towel.

"Girls, is everything okay?" Mrs. Willis called from the living room.

"Yes, ma'am." Sam nodded at the scanner and asked Makayla, "Can you grab that?"

"Sure." Makayla took the scanner, carried it into the living room, and set it on the coffee table.

Sam followed, hugging the poor little kitten.

"What's that you have?" Mrs. Willis asked.

"A kitten I found next to your house." Sam knelt beside the chair and showed Mrs. Willis. "Do you know who it belongs to?"

"No idea. Poor little thing looks like it's been abandoned."

Sam snuggled the kitten. "It's almost frozen." She looked at Makayla. "Turn the scanner on. Maybe we can get an update about Mom."

Makayla turned on the scanner. Chewy barked outside. "I'll let her back in." She headed into the kitchen. Chewy beat her back to the living room, shaking and sending pellets of sleet all over the couch.

"Chewy!" Sam said.

The dog ignored any reprimand, nosing toward the kitten Sam held. Chewy put her nose against the kitten's wet head. The kitten wobbled to standing. Chewy sniffed at the kitten, who hissed and popped Chewy on the nose. The dog jumped back.

Sam laughed. "Even scrawny and freezing, she's got guts." She nuzzled the kitten. Chewy laid on the rug, staring at Sam and the kitten with cautious eyes. At least the kitten had helped stop her over-active imagination.

"Listen," Mrs. Willis said, leaning over to turn up the volume on the scanner.

"All passengers are accounted for," a female voice came from the scanner.

"Copy that. Twelve are en route to hospital. Twenty-two receiving EMT care onsite," a male's voice responded.

"Fire is contained."

"Affirmative. No casualties," the man's voice boomed.

No casualties! That meant Mom was . . . the tight hold around Sam's heart released. She could breathe normally again.

"Woohoo!" Makayla hugged Sam.

Chewy barked.

"Thank you, Jesus," Mrs. Willis whispered.

Sam snuggled the kitten. Mom might be one of the ones hurt, but she was alive!

Thanks, God.

Mrs. Willis turned down the scanner. "Now, what are we going to do about this kitten?"

"We can't put her back outside." Sam let the kitten go. On wobbly legs, she stepped off the beach towel.

Chewy approached slowly, then lay down right in front of the kitten. The kitten sniffed Chewy, then plopped down right beside the dog.

"I think she likes you, Chewy." Sam reached out and ran her fingers over her dog's smooth muzzle. "Sweet girl, Chewy."

"I guess the kitten will stay put until your parents get home, Sam." Mrs. Willis sat back on the recliner. "I think that fire needs stirring, and maybe another log."

"Yes, ma'am. I'll get it." Sam headed out to the garage to grab a log from the rack Dad had just filled last weekend.

Even though she now knew Mom was safe, she still had a funny taste in her mouth. And, now that she thought about it, taking into consideration the fear she'd just felt, some things didn't feel as incredibly important as they had before. Like the virus. And Felicia's expulsion.

Although, Sam *did* wonder again how Aubrey found out about Felicia's expulsion.

Sam lifted two logs and headed back into the house, still mulling things over. Captain York sure noticed Sam's article pretty quickly after she posted it. Almost like he'd been waiting for it. But why? He was a boss with the Little Rock Police Department, which meant he had a lot more important things to do.

"Oh, thank you, dear." Mrs. Willis hoisted herself from the recliner. "I'm going to the ladies' room."

Sam poked the fire, then put one of the logs on top.

She closed the protective screen and stood in front of it, letting the heat seep into her bones.

"It's okay to still be worrying about your mom, you know." Makayla lay on her stomach, wiggling her fingers to play with the kitten.

"I know. I hope she's not one of the injured ones, but I know she's safe. I'm all right."

"Then what are you tossing around in that mind of yours?" Makayla sat up, leaning her back against the arm of the couch. "I can almost see the wheels turning from down here."

Sam grinned, but plopped down on the rug and rubbed Chewy's belly. "I'm trying to figure out how Captain York knew about my article going up so quickly after I posted it. I mean, it was only — what? Maybe ten or fifteen minutes at the most? Was he sitting on the site, watching? He's a cop and it's a busy time with the weather. It doesn't add up."

"Right. I guess I didn't think about it." Makayla laughed as the kitten tripped over her own feet and rolled on the rug.

A thought occurred to Sam. "You know, I just thought of a way I might be able to find out who told Aubrey about Felicia."

"Yeah?"

"Nikki Cole. She might be willing to clue me in. Because you know Aubrey bragged to Nikki how she was able to scoop me."

"Good thinking." Makayla nodded. "She's been much nicer to you since you helped her with the bullying thing."

"It's worth a try."

"I'd say so."

"Girls, can I get you anything?" Mrs. Willis came back into the living room.

"No, ma'am," Sam said.

Sam's cell phone rang. She noticed from the caller-ID that it was her father and quickly snatched it up. "Dad?"

"Hey, my girl." Mom's voice never sounded so sweet.

"Mom!"

"Now, I'm sure you were scared, but don't you worry, I'm fine. Just got a little bump on my head. They want Dad to take me to the emergency room just to make sure I don't have a concussion. I'm certain I don't, but you know how Dad can be."

Sam smiled even though tears wet her cheeks. "Yeah, I know how he can be." She sniffed.

"I'm okay, Sam. Really. Dad's going to take me to the hospital, then we'll be home."

"Okay."

"All right, my sweet girl, here's Dad. I love you."

"I love you too, Mom."

"Sam?" Dad's voice sounded relieved.

She sniffed again. "Hey, Dad."

"I'm just going to take her to get checked out, but with the weather, it might take us a while. Are you okay?"

"We're fine." The kitten pushed Sam's hand with her nose. "We'll keep the fire going."

"That's my girl. Let me talk to Mrs. Willis."

"Okay. Hey, Dad?"

"Yeah, pumpkin?"

"I love you."

"I love you too." The smile was in his voice.

"Here's Mrs. Willis." She handed the phone to her neighbor, then whispered to Makayla what the other side of the conversation had been.

"You just take your time, Charles. Me and the girls are just fine." Mrs. Willis handed Sam back her iPhone. "I don't know how to turn it off."

Sam laughed. "It's okay. It turns off when the call is ended."

"It's wonderful about your mother being okay."

"Yes, ma'am, it is." Sam couldn't stop smiling.

Sam's message alert sounded. She glanced at the message. "Hey, they say power should be restored within the hour." She glanced at the kitten curled up by Chewy. "I need to find some kitty litter and a box for her."

"I believe I have some in my garage," Mrs. Willis said.

"You have a litter box and litter in your garage?" Sam blurted out. "You don't have a cat."

Mrs. Willis chuckled. "No, I don't, but I cat-sit for the Hardens from time to time, so I keep a litter box and litter. It's in the cabinet by the door if you want to use it."

"Thank you. I'll get it right now." Sam bundled up and ran next door, returning with the items. She set them up in the laundry room. "Thank you, Mrs. Willis. Once Mom and Dad get home and we decide what to do with Baby Kitty, I'll clean it out and return it."

"No rush, dear." She let out a long sigh. "I think I'm going to lay back here in this comfy recliner and rest my eyes a bit, if you girls don't mind."

"You know what, Mrs. Willis ... a friend of ours lives just a few blocks over and I'd love to go visit her. Why don't I put the kitten in the laundry room and take Chewy with us? That way, you can rest a bit."

"Sure, dear. That's so thoughtful."

Sam quickly put the kitten in the laundry room, set out a bowl of water and a bowl of milk, then found Chewy's leash. She was already bundled up and waiting on Makayla. "Hurry up." She was ready to go to see Nikki Cole.

She was ready for answers.

CHAPTER FIFTEEN

"Hi Jefferson. Is Nikki here?" Sam stood on the front porch while Makayla stood in the driveway, holding Chewy's leash. Maybe she should have called first to make sure Nikki was home. It'd just be her luck for Nikki to be gone. Like at Aubrey's or something.

At least it wasn't sleeting any more, but it'd gotten colder. The sun would be down soon, and then it'd really get cold. Sam had promised Mrs. Willis they'd be back before it got dark.

"Yeah, hang on." He turned from the door and hollered, "Nikki, you got company again." He turned back to Sam and Makayla. "Y'all want to come inside? The electricity's off, but we have the fire going."

"Our electricity's out too." Sam shifted her weight

SAMANTHA SANDERSON OFF THE RECORD

from one foot to the other. "But I got an alert that it should be back on within an hour."

"That's cool. Y'all been sledding? Nikki and her friends went early this morning, before it started sleeting."

"No, we haven't gone sledding yet. Just had a snowball fight and played around."

"That's cool."

Nikki appeared behind her brother. "Hey, Sam. Makayla. What are you doing here?"

"We were walking Chewy and thought we'd drop by and say hello." Sam smiled. "Want to come out and walk with us for a bit?"

Nikki looked at Sam, then Makayla, then back at Sam. "Sure. Why not? Let me tell Mom and get my coat and boots. Hang on." She shut the door and disappeared.

Sam went down the porch steps and petted Chewy.

"I still feel funny being here. Asking her and all," Makayla whispered.

"It'll be fine. She either knows or she doesn't. She'll either tell us or she won't."

The door opened and Nikki bounced down the stairs. She had auburn hair like her brother, and she was tall for a girl her age, but slender. She and Aubrey were best friends, but ever since Sam had gotten to know Nikki a little bit better, for the life of her, she couldn't figure out why Nikki was friends with someone like Aubrey.

Nikki joined them on the driveway. "Okay, what's going on?"

CHAPTER FIFTEEN

"I need a favor." Sam led them down the driveway to the sidewalk.

"What kind of favor?"

"Have you seen the school's blog today?"

"No. I've been outside most of the morning and then the power went off."

"Well, first off, Aubrey posted a story that implied an unnamed transfer student was to blame for the virus."

Nikki nodded and ran her teeth over her bottom lip. "I knew about that."

"How'd you know?"

"Aubrey told me this morning. She said she was going to scoop you."

"I guess you know who the person Aubrey referred to is?"

Nikki nodded. "Yep. Felicia Adams."

"Well, I already knew about Felicia. I knew the whole truth, which was why I didn't post an article about it."

Nikki narrowed her eyes. "You, Sam Sanderson, held back on a story?"

Was it so hard to believe she'd not print a story to protect a friend? She stared at Nikki's face. Obviously it was.

"I didn't write a story about it because I knew Felicia didn't tamper with any grades at Pulaski Academy."

"Then Aubrey was given wrong information? That wasn't what Felicia was expelled for?"

"It was, but she didn't do it."

Nikki smiled, but it was as cold as the snow on the ground. "Sam. Seriously? You're the one who usually reports the facts, no matter what. You're telling me you let Aubrey scoop you because Felicia said she didn't do what Pulaski Academy listed as the reason for her expulsion? Because why? Felicia said she didn't tamper with any grades? And you, Sam Sanderson, of all people, believed her?" She crossed her arms over her chest.

"It's not like that." Why was Nikki acting so ... so much like Aubrey? Just yesterday she'd apologized for the way Aubrey treated Sam and took part of the blame.

"I'm confused, Sam. Why are you here?"

"Why are you being so mean?" Sam asked, confused. It hurt her feelings that Nikki, who she'd thought had been a sorta-kinda friend, had such a flipped attitude from yesterday.

Makayla stood in silence, her gaze bouncing back and forth between Sam and Nikki.

Nikki shook her head. "I-I ... I'm sorry. I just got off the phone with Aubrey. I was actually on the phone with her when you got here."

"Oh." Sam didn't know what to say. What did that have to do with the way Nikki was acting? Was Aubrey's ugly attitude rubbing off on Nikki?

"I was with her this morning and she was on cloud nine because she was going to scoop you. Now, she's furious with you something awful. She just spent at least twenty minutes ranting and raving about you. Asking me how I could have ever been nice to you. Telling me that you just had to do something to try and scoop her back. And on and on and on." Nikki lifted the collar of her coat around her neck. "I guess I was just taking my frustration out on you. I'm sorry."

"It's okay. I can only imagine what she said." Probably some of the same stuff Sam said about Aubrey.

Nikki grinned. "No, you really can't."

"Oh. I see." Sam smiled, but it was a little unnerving to realize that someone really disliked her that much. It also hurt her feelings more than a little that everyone seemed to think she'd report on a story to get a scoop, even if it meant hurting a friend.

"So, what's your favor?"

Sam glanced at Makayla, then back at Nikki. "Do you know who told Aubrey about Felicia's expulsion?"

Nikki's eyes went wide. "You don't know who told her?"

Sam shook her head.

"Oh." Nikki looked conflicted.

Sam regretted asking her. After hearing about Mom's incident ... well, it just made Sam think about things a little differently. Like how people are more important than a story, even if it could make a career. Why, if someone asked Sam to betray Makayla, she wouldn't. Not for anything. Despite what she thought of Aubrey, Nikki and Aubrey were best friends.

"I'm sorry, Nikki. That's not fair. I shouldn't have asked you. Aubrey's your best friend, and I'm asking you to betray her confidence. I'm sorry. I shouldn't have come. Forget I asked." She took Chewy's leash from Makayla. "Enjoy the rest of your snow day. I hope your power comes back on soon." She turned back toward her street.

"Sam," Nikki said.

She turned around and faced Nikki. "No, it was wrong of me to ask. I shouldn't have."

"It's not like I'd be betraying her. I was standing right there when he told her this morning while we were sledding down Chenal Valley's big hill."

"Who?"

"Doug. Doug York."

Sam locked stares with Makayla, then looked back at Nikki. "Doug York told you and Aubrey that Felicia had been expelled from Pulaski Academy for grade tampering?" This was incredible.

Nikki nodded. "Yeah. I didn't know he'd gone to Pulaski Academy, did you? He did up until this year when his dad made him transfer to Robinson because he decided it didn't look right for a cop's son to attend a private school. Him being a public servant and all."

What a load of lies! Sam pressed her lips together to keep from blurting out that Doug had been failing. She couldn't break Dad's trust, but man, this was crazy. Wasn't it more important to defend a person's reputation? People *were* more important than stories.

Nikki didn't notice anything, and she continued on. "Anyway, he said he'd been there when the investigation went down. He left just before she was expelled, but his friends who were still there told him that's why she came to Robinson."

"That's what he said?" Why would he try to point suspicion at Felicia? What did he have against her?

Nikki nodded. "Yep. I heard him myself."

Before Sam could reply, Nikki's cell phone went off. She glanced at the caller-ID. "It's Aubrey."

"You'd better take it, or she'll get mad. Thanks for the info." Sam looped her arm through Makayla's and started off toward her street even as she tugged gently on Chewy's leash.

"Bye." Nikki took off her glove and tapped her touch screen. "Hi Aubrey. No, just outside. What's up?"

Sam remained silent until they were out of earshot of Nikki. She sure didn't want Aubrey to hear her voice over the phone. They turned off the connecting street onto Sam's.

"Can you believe him?" Sam exclaimed. "He's the one who tells Aubrey, knowing she'd use the information to try and one-up me, then his dad calls my dad because he's upset about the article Aubrey wrote."

"That's messed up." Makayla shook her head.

"I know. What's his deal? Why would he do that? You know him better than I do. What do you think?"

"I don't know him that well. We just have computer

science together. Maybe he and Felicia have some differences," Makayla suggested. "Has Felicia said anything about him?"

"Not that I recall." Sam tried to figure it out. Nothing made sense.

While the sun hadn't been out today, darkness eased over the capitol city, stealing the light from the sky as night settled in. The wind stirred, kicking up snow and blowing it about. Coldness shoved around in the air.

They stomped their boots before going in through the garage. "We're back, Mrs. Willis," Sam called out, then hung up her coat. The house was much cooler than it'd been earlier.

The kitten welcomed them with a steady series of *meows* as they opened the laundry room door.

"Well, don't you sound stronger?" Sam picked her up and nuzzled her under her chin, then handed her to Makayla. "Come on, Chewy, let me get you dried off." She used the old towel to dry the German hunt terrier's thick black and brown fur.

Once they were all dry, the two girls and two animals joined Mrs. Willis in the living room. "You barely made it back before nightfall. Did you have a nice walk?"

"We did. Did you get some rest?" Sam asked as she moved to the kitchen and refilled Chewy's water bowl.

"I did a little reading." Mrs. Willis stood and stretched. "But I think I let the fire go out."

"I'll rebuild it." Sam used part of a starter log and

the three pieces of wood Makayla brought in from the garage. Within minutes, a roaring fire heated the room. "There. That's better."

As if on cue, the electricity came back on.

Mrs. Willis clapped. "Lovely." She glanced out the window. "Girls, I need to run back to my house for a few moments and make sure everything's okay. Will you be all right if I'm gone for a few minutes?"

"Sure. Take your time." Sam sat on the hearth beside Makayla, smiling at Baby Kitty, as she thought of her, who was playing with Chewy's wagging tail.

Makayla stretched out on her stomach on the rug. "So, what are you going to do about Doug York and Felicia? Are you going to tell your dad that Doug was the one who told Aubrey about Felicia?"

"I don't know yet. Maybe. Probably. I just want to know what his end game is."

"I can't help you there. You're the one with the super ninja deduction skills."

"Right." Sam snapped her fingers and pointed. "I'm going to find out." She jumped up and went to the desk, pulled open the top drawer, and rummaged through the massive junk items.

"What are you looking for? What are you going to do?"

"I'm looking for the school directory. I'm calling Doug York."

CHAPTER SIXTEEN

A re you sure you want to call him? What are you going to say?" Makayla stretched out on Sam's bed, watching Sam pace as she held her phone.

"I have to. I need to find out why Doug told Aubrey about Felicia, knowing Aubrey would put it in an article. I owe it to Felicia."

They'd left Mrs. Willis reading the newspaper in the living room and taken Chewy and Baby Kitty into Sam's room.

"Okay, but be careful. Remember, his dad is your dad's boss."

"I know." Sam dialed the number listed for him in the school directory, silently hoping it was Doug's cell phone number and not a landline that his dad might answer.

"Hello," a woman's voice answered.

No such luck on it being his cell phone, but at least Captain York hadn't answered. Sam cleared her throat. "Is Doug available?"

"Yes he is. May I ask who's calling?"

If she gave her name, and Captain York was there, it'd be bad. Sam improvised. "Makayla. Makayla Ansley from school."

Mac rolled over and threw a pillow at Sam's head.

"Just a moment, Makayla."

Sam looked at Mac and mouthed "sorry."

Makayla wagged a finger in front of her face.

"Hello?"

"Doug?" Sam activated the *Call Recorder* app on her phone that would record their conversation.

"Yeah? Makayla?"

"Uh, no. This is Sam."

"Who?"

Her mouth went dry. Maybe she should have listened to Makayla. "Um, you know, Sam Sanderson. From school."

"Yeah, I know who you are. What do you want?"

Makayla shook her head.

Sam ignored her. "I want to know why you told Aubrey Damas that Felicia Adams was expelled from Pulaski Academy for grade tampering."

Makayla fell back on the bed and pulled a pillow over her head.

"What? Who told you I said that?"

"You're going to deny it? Really?"

"Hang on," he practically growled. A minute passed. Two.

"Okay. Now, who told you I said anything?"

"So you aren't denying it?"

"No. It's the truth."

"No it isn't. Felicia didn't tamper with any grades."

"That's not what the records say."

Sam sank into her chair. "How do you know what her records say?"

"I went to PA."

Something wasn't right. The timeline didn't work. "Yeah, but you would've already left PA and come to Robinson before Felicia was expelled." That was it! "You were here a good couple of months before Felicia."

"I heard about it from my friends at PA. Duh."

Duh? No. He'd gotten it from his father — she'd bet her Panda hat on it. "Really, Doug? Who?"

"I don't have to tell you."

"No, you don't, but you know I don't believe that any friend told you." It didn't even matter how he knew. What mattered is why he'd told Aubrey.

"What's your point, Sanderson?"

"My point is why did you tell Aubrey? Why would you sic her on Felicia?"

"That's none of your business." He was downright snippy.

Which irritated her all the more. Sam moved fully into an attitude. It was time someone stood up for the Felicias of the world ... and Dad too. "It is my business when your dad calls my dad, accusing me of being involved."

"Sam!" Makayla hissed. "Are you crazy?"

Sam shushed her with a hand. "Doug?"

"Look, just stop sticking your nose where it doesn't belong." Doug's tone had gotten sharp and carried more than a hint of anger.

"All I want to know is why? What did Felicia ever do to you?"

"Nothing." That one word ... his voice lowered a little bit.

She softened her tone, and her delivery. "Then why tell Aubrey? Why give her the information?"

He was silent. Then it hit her. Maybe none of this was about Felicia. Or Aubrey. Maybe it was about *her*.

Sam kept her tone very soft and very low. "Because you wanted Aubrey to scoop me? Is that it?" She held her breath. Was it possible that she'd unintentionally hurt him in some way?

"You always seem to know everything, Sanderson. It's annoying. Especially because they wouldn't let me on the paper. Even knowing who my dad is, they wouldn't let me on." Doug's hateful tone had returned with even more anger.

Sam grabbed her throw pillow, the one Makayla had

hurled at her head earlier, and gripped it tight against her chest. He'd hurt someone else to hurt *her*? Felicia and Dad both because Doug had a problem with Sam? "So this was to get back at me? To give Aubrey something to use that you thought I didn't have? For what?"

"Aubrey said if I helped her, she'd put in a good word for me with Mrs. Pape and Mrs. Trees. Recommend me for the newspaper."

That conniving Aubrey ... "Doug, don't you know Aubrey well enough to know that she was only using you?"

"You're just mad because she scooped you."

"Doug, Doug, Doug ... I scooped her today. The virus has been removed. Everything's been restored. My dad told your dad. Your dad even called Mrs. Trees to tell her the good news."

"You're such a liar, just like Aubrey says."

Sam's anger flared, and she couldn't help herself from blurting out her thoughts. "Didn't your daddy tell you?"

Oops, there went that love your neighbor resolution.

"You're lying, Sanderson."

"Really? Check out the paper's blog. It's all there."

Chewy rushed to the door, barking. Her parents must be home.

"I've got to go, Doug. I'd suggest you tell your father everything ... what you've done. I'm telling mine, and

I'm sure it's only a matter of time before your dad asks you about it. Goodbye." She ended the call, then emailed herself a copy of the recorded call.

"Sam?" Mom's voice drifted down the hall.

Sam tossed her phone on her bed and opened the door. Chewy darted into the hall, jumping and wagging her tail. Sam met her mother in the hallway. She stepped into her mom's arms, holding her tight. The comforting scent of Coco by Chanel, Mom's trademark perfume, brought Sam an immediate sense of peace.

Mom kissed her head. "It's okay. I'm fine. The hospital says I don't have a concussion. Just a little bump on the noggin where I was resting my head on the seat in front of me."

Dad's voice and Mrs. Willis's came from the living room, but Sam didn't want to listen to them right now. All she cared about was that Mom was home. Safe. Sam hugged her a little tighter. "I'm glad you're okay, Mom." She couldn't stop the trembling of her legs as she closed her eyes and held her mother a little longer before letting her go.

"I am too, my girl."

Makayla stepped out of the bedroom into the hall. "Hello, Mrs. Sanderson. I'm glad you're home safely."

"Hi, Makayla. I'm so glad you were here with Sam." She pulled Makayla into her hug.

Baby Kitty wobbled into the hall. *Meow.*

Mom's eyes widened. "Oh. Who is this?"

Sam scooped her up, nuzzling her. "Mom, this is Baby Kitty. I found her out in the sleet. She was practically frozen." She held the kitten out to her mom. "Baby Kitty, this is Mom."

Mom took the kitten and held it close. Baby Kitty lifted her head and licked the end of Mom's chin, making Mom giggle.

Yeah, we are so getting to keep the kitten now.

"I need to rest now. I'm really tired from all the excitement today." She handed Baby Kitty back to Sam and kissed Sam's forehead. "I'll talk to you girls in the morning."

"Okay. Uh, Mom?"

"Yes, sweet girl?"

"You are going to take a shower, right?"

She chuckled. "Yes, Sam, I'll wash all the germs off me before I go to bed." She headed to the master bedroom.

"I'll let Chewy out," Makayla volunteered.

"Okay. Thanks." Sam went into the living room where Mrs. Willis was putting on her coat.

"I'm going to walk Mrs. Willis home," Dad said.

Sam hugged their neighbor. "Thanks for being here today. And for letting me listen to the scanner." The *love your neighbor* thing seemed to be a two-way street. Especially a neighbor that Sam realized she really loved.

"You're most welcome, dear." She started for the

garage. "And you keep that litter box for as long as you need it."

Dad looked Sam. "Litter box?"

Sam smiled. "I'll explain when you get back."

"I'm sure." He followed Mrs. Willis into the garage.

Sam went into the kitchen and let Chewy back in. Makayla stood in front of the pantry. "Okay, girl, I'm hungry. Those grilled cheese sandwiches and soup were too many hours ago. My stomach is a-rumbling."

"Peanut butter and jelly?"

"And chocolate milk?" Makayla sounded hopeful.

"Of course."

"Sold!"

The girls had just finished making their spontaneous dinner when Sam's father returned from next door. "Those look good," he said.

"I'll make you a couple." Sam hopped up and pulled out another plate.

"Thanks." He grabbed the milk jug and poured. "I'm sorry I couldn't take you with me today, Sam."

"I understand. I didn't like it, but I understood." And it'd given her time to think. Time to realize what was really important in life: the people that you love.

"Good." He put the milk back in the refrigerator. "Pretty slick of you to get Mrs. Willis to let you listen in on the scanner."

"Good thing too. That's how we found out there were no casualties." She turned and smiled at him. "Two peanut butter and jellies, with butter, just the way you like them."

They sat at the table and Dad offered grace, then the three of them ate.

"Do you think Mom would like a sandwich?" Sam asked.

"I think your mom is very tired and just wants a hot shower and a warm bed."

Sam nodded. "Dad. About Captain York?"

"Don't worry about it, Sam. I'll talk to him tomorrow. You tried and that's all I could ask of you."

"I found out who told Aubrey about Felicia."

"You did? She called you back?" He took a big bite of his sandwich.

"No, I went to ask Aubrey's best friend, and found out she was with Aubrey when she learned about Felicia."

"So who told her?"

"Doug York. Your boss's son."

"What?" Dad coughed, nearly choking. He took a long drink of milk. "Are you sure?"

"I am. And so I called Doug myself, to verify."

"Sam ..."

"No, it's okay. He wouldn't admit that he got the information on Felicia from his father, but he did admit that he told Aubrey and that he did it so she could scoop me. Oh, and he wants to be on the paper so Aubrey told him she'd put in a good word for him with Mrs. Pape and Mrs. Trees."

"Sam."

"I told him I was going to tell you, so I suggested he tell his father before you had a chance to talk to his dad."

"I'm assuming it's your word against his, as usual?"

"Not exactly."

"Do tell?"

"I recorded it with an app and sent a copy of the recording to my computer. For backup purposes only."

"Well. I guess I'll call my captain in the morning. I might need a copy of that recording."

Sam took the last bite of her sandwich and drank the rest of her chocolate milk to wash it down. She'd call Felicia tonight and let her know. And apologize again, because even though she didn't tell Aubrey about Felicia's expulsion, Aubrey was told because of her — because Doug wanted to prove Sam didn't always know everything.

Now the only thing left for her to figure out was who created the virus and infected their system. And why.

But Dad apparently had something else he wanted figured out. "Now, what's the story about that litter box?"

CHAPTER SEVENTEEN

I'll call you later." Makayla gave Sam another quick hug before following Sam's dad into the truck the next morning.

Sam's dad slowly pulled out of the driveway. Sam waved one last time at her bestie before heading back into the house. She wandered into the kitchen where Mom was enjoying a cup of coffee, Baby Kitty playing at her feet.

"I'm glad Dad's going to let us keep her." Sam pulled out the chair across the table and sat. "I was afraid he might not."

"Ah, your dad likes to come across as gruff and tough, but he's a softie. Baby Kitty jumped up on the bed this morning and snuggled with him. He's pretty much sold on her." Mom smiled.

Sam reached down and wiggled her fingers at the kitten. "She already looks stronger. You wouldn't believe how scrawny and sickly she looked when I found her. I didn't know if she was a big rat or a kitten until she meowed."

"Sam, I want to talk to you about the accident." Mom's tone was serious.

Sam felt a little sick inside. "It's okay, Mom. You're home. You're fine. It's all good."

"No, it's not." Mom traced the rim of her coffee cup. "It was scary. For me. For Dad. For you."

Sam nodded, not trusting herself to speak. She didn't want to ever be that scared again.

"I appreciate you trying to be brave, but I can only imagine how scared you must have been."

All these crazy feelings and thoughts that Sam didn't even realize were inside of her suddenly bubbled out. "You go on dangerous assignments all the time, a whole lot more dangerous than an airplane ride, but I've never been so scared you would get hurt or . . ."

"Or die?" Mom's voice was very soft.

Sam nodded. She took a deep breath before she continued. "I know you told me that every day you pray for God to hold me and Dad in His hands, and you mentally picture putting us there. And I've done that a lot since you told me. You're right, it does help me not worry so much because I know there's no better place for you to be. But. Yesterday." She shook her head. "I couldn't hold on to the picture in my head. I kept seeing every picture or report I've ever seen of a plane crash. Fire and explosions." She shuddered. "It was horrible."

Her mom reached across the table and took her hand. "I know. I did the same thing."

"You did?" Mom? Sam never thought of her mom ever being scared.

"I did. When we started sliding, I know it happened fast, but it felt like everything was in slow motion."

"Did your life pass before your eyes like everyone says it does?" Sam's eyes were wide.

Mom gave a little laugh. "No. Mine didn't. But I kept seeing your face and your dad's. And then I'd imagine the plane catching on fire. I wanted to keep thinking of you and Dad, but the mental image of a fire kept pushing your faces out of my mind."

"Thanks, Mom." Sam smiled so her mother would understand.

Her mother chuckled. "Well, it's the truth. In those few minutes that felt like forever, I was praying and praying for God to not take me from you and your dad. I want to see you grow up. I want to grow old with your father."

Tears filled Sam's eyes, and she wasn't really sure why.

"And while I was praying, do you know what I realized?"

Sam shook her head, not trusting herself to speak. She was pretty sure she'd start bawling if she tried.

Mom squeezed her hand. "One particular Scripture kept coming to my mind. Deuteronomy 31:6. *'Be strong and courageous. Do not fear or be in dread of them, for it is the Lord your God who goes with you. He will not leave you or forsake you.'* And then I realized, I'm not alone. No matter what. And neither are you or your dad. God will always be with all of us, no matter what."

"That's good, Mom, but I was scared of losing you. Of never seeing you again." Tears rolled down her face.

Mom stood and came around the table and drew Sam into her arms. "I was scared too." She hugged Sam so tight that Sam thought she might not be able to breathe, then released her hold. She put her fingers under Sam's chin and lifted her face to look her in the eye. "But we will not, cannot, let fear stop us from living. Yes, we should use caution and common sense and not be reckless, but we aren't going to shy away from life."

Sam nodded.

Mom searched her face. "Do you really understand what I'm saying?"

"I think so."

Baby Kitty spied Chewy drinking from her water bowl. She started running, jumping at Chewy, who was startled and took off. Baby Kitty gave chase.

Sam smiled.

"Just like Baby Kitty," Mom said.

What? Sam looked at her mom and raised her eyebrows. "I don't follow."

"Baby Kitty was abandoned in a nasty mix of winter weather. Cold. Wet. Alone. She could have easily died had you not been out there at that exact time and heard her. She was facing certain death before you intervened. You saved her."

Sam thought about the pitiful lump of fur Baby Kitty had been when she discovered her out in the snow. Wet and looking more like a drowned rat than a fluffy kitten. "Right." Sam nodded.

"Now, she has every reason to be fearful of everything. Scared of any and everything. But instead, she's pouncing on my slippers. Jumping up on the bed and kneading Dad's chest. Chasing a dog five times her size. She's not letting fear guide her life."

"Oh. I get it."

"I want us to be like Baby Kitty. Yes, our past should change us, but we shouldn't live in fear." Mom lifted her coffee cup. "I'm going to get another cup. Do you want me to make you some hot chocolate?"

"No, thanks."

Mom refilled her mug.

Sam thought about how she'd felt when faced with maybe losing her mom, and then how she'd realized how people were more important than stories or scoops.

"Hey, Mom, can I ask you something." Sam leaned

against the bar adjacent to the counter with the coffee pot.

"Sure."

"How do you figure out what you should report on and what you shouldn't?"

"Well, I'm normally sent on an assignment."

"No, I mean, what angle to take." She wasn't being very clear. "I mean, how do you decide if what you're reporting, while it's true, is worth the chance of someone getting hurt? Someone innocent." Because people were more important. They *had* to be.

"That's always a tough call." Mom poured a little more cream into her coffee, then added another spoon of sugar. "I try to ask myself if what I'm reporting is of greater benefit to many. If I think what I report might hurt someone innocent, I try to find another way of reporting. Sometimes, it's just not possible and I have to get the story out there because it's important for the public." She took a sip of coffee. "All I can tell you is to learn to trust yourself and your judgment. Let your conscience be your guide." She smiled. "I know that's so lame, but it's true. Can't help it."

And Sam's conscience happened to sound just like Makayla. All the time.

● ● ●

"Well, if it isn't Samantha Sanderson."

Sam didn't even bother to turn around. She wiped

her mouth and straightened in front of the water fountain. "Aubrey Damas." Sam plastered a smile on her face and turned around. "How are you?"

The snow had melted off a few hours ago, so it seemed everyone was out and about this Saturday morning. But of all the grocery stores in a city as big as Little Rock . . . what were the odds of being in the exact same one at the exact same time as Aubrey?

Man, her luck stunk. If this was any indication of how her new year would be, she'd just as soon skip it.

No, she needed to face it. Head on. No more not dealing with this.

"I bet you think you're really on top of the world with your latest article, don't you?" Aubrey hissed.

She will not get to me. I will love my neighbor. Even if this *particular* neighbor made her want to kill said neighbor. She would resist. "No, Aubrey. I'm just doing my job. That's all."

"Uh-huh. Like I believe that."

Sam bit her tongue, determined not to let anger get the best of her. Not today. She swallowed and stared at the girl who she'd been friends with back in elementary school. What had happened to change all that?

"Aubrey, I don't know what I've done to offend you, and I'm not being sarcastic. I'm really not. I have no idea what I ever did to you, but I'm sorry if I've hurt you or anything." Wow, amazing. She didn't choke on her tongue.

It was a New Year's miracle.

"Stop being smart, Samantha." But Aubrey looked unsure of herself.

"I'm not. Seriously. No teasing, no sarcasm. Whatever I did, I really am sorry." And she was. She meant the apology.

Aubrey stared at her. Hard. "If you don't know, then you can't be sorry for it." She put her hand on her hip and did that little swaying thing of hers. And she smirked.

Sam hated that smirk. She'd apologized and meant it, but she couldn't make Aubrey accept it.

"You know what, Aubrey, you're right. I don't know, so I can't be sorry for something specific. But it's obvious I've done something sometime that either hurt you or made you mad or offended you. I might not know what, specifically, but what I do know is I've never intentionally tried to hurt you or offend you." She had, on several occasions, tried to make her mad, so Sam opted not to include that. Loving her neighbor had to be done in stages. Right now, this was the best she could do.

"You can either accept my apology or not. You can tell me what your problem is or not. Either way, my conscience is clear and I'm all good." She smiled at Aubrey, who for once seemed totally speechless. After a couple of seconds of silence, Sam decided to make her exit. "Have a great Saturday. I'll see you at school on Monday."

Walking back to meet Mom, Sam smiled.

CHAPTER EIGHTEEN

Dad parked the truck and turned off the engine. Sam was out in a flash. "See y'all after Sunday school," she told her parents before running toward the youth room, iPad under her arm.

West Little Rock Christian Church stood off Highway 10, drawing attention with its beautiful and oversized stained glass front. Sam had always been mesmerized by the depiction of Jesus in the bright yellow, gold, and alabaster pieces of stained glass.

Sam didn't know how old the church was, but she'd been attending since she was born. It was like a second home to her.

Sam ran down the hallway toward the special youth room. Last year, the youth group had come together to redesign their room. They'd painted it white with stripes in green, purple, and blue. The couch cushions matched the green and blue, and the bean bag chairs were purple. Sam's favorite part of the room was the verse painted on the wall:

> Don't let anyone think less
> of you because YOU ARE young.
> Be AN EXAMPLE to all believers
> in what you teach,
> IN THE WAY YOU LIVE, in your love,
> YOUR FAITH, and your purity.
>
> 1 Timothy 4:12

Sam rushed into the room, anxious to tell Makayla about her run-in with Aubrey. Sam hadn't been able to fill Mac in because she, Mom, and Dad had played board games last night. The rule at the house was during game time phones were to be turned off.

Stepping into the room, Sam saw that her best friend was already there, but she was with some guy Sam had never seen before.

He was tall, probably close to six feet, but way thin. His skin was really pale but looked even paler because his hair was so blond it was almost white. It was obvious the boy didn't stay out in the sun for very long.

Makayla smiled as she caught sight of her. She pulled the guy along with her. "Sam, I want you to meet my friend, David. He's in the computer research demographic group with me. David, this is my bestest friend, Sam Sanderson. Sam's the star of our school newspaper."

Blushing, Sam shook David's hand. "She's trying to embarrass me. Nice to meet you."

"You too. Makayla talks about you all the time."

"She probably exaggerates."

"It's all good," he said with a smile. Even his teeth were eerily white.

"Oh. Then it's all true. Every word of it."

"Funny." Makayla shook her head. "David's regular church had some roof damage from the ice, so Mom invited his family to come to church with us."

"Welcome. I'm happy to finally meet someone in Mac's group." She leaned over to him and used a stage whisper voice. "I was beginning to think the whole group was just a figment of her imagination."

"Oh, you're really funny today, aren't you?" Makayla smiled.

Sam, David, and Makayla went to go sit down, and Sam pulled her tablet out of her shoulder bag. As she tapped the Bible app on her iPad, she noticed David pulled a real Bible from his backpack. As he did, she saw a USB drive on the backpack's zipper. It looked vaguely familiar. It was in the shape of a key, but had a really cool zebra head on it.

Where had she seen it before?

Ms. Martha stood and opened the group with a prayer. Then she lifted her head and welcomed the visitors. Sam smiled as she noticed the little bulge of Ms. Martha's belly. Not too long ago, the youth director had shared that she and her husband were going to have their first baby in May.

"Instead of going over a specific Scripture today, I thought I'd ask if any of you took my suggestion to find a Scripture and to base one of your new year's resolutions on it. If you did, I would love for some of you to share which one and how you're doing so far."

Daniel, the high school guy who was always so nice to everyone, spoke up. "I selected Proverbs 3:27: 'Do not withhold good from those to whom it is due, when it is in your power to act.'"

"That's a good one." Ms. Martha nodded. "How're you doing with it so far?"

"Pretty good. I'm looking for reasons to compliment someone or give them kudos, instead of not saying anything. Like, last week, we went to a restaurant and the waiter was really, really good. Instead of only leaving him a nice tip, I asked to see the manager on our way out. I told the manager how the waiter had given us such great service and I just wanted him to know. The manager thanked me and even told me that he was going to make a note in the waiter's file so it would be there for his next employee evaluation."

"Very good, Daniel. Thank you for sharing." Ms. Martha looked around. "Anybody else?"

Ava Kate, a fellow seventh grader, raised her hand. "I chose Matthew 5:4: 'Blessed are those who mourn, for they will be comforted.'"

Ms. Martha sat back in her chair. "Interesting. How are you doing with it?"

"Well, I talked with my mother about it after you suggested it, and she's helping me. We make little lap afghans together and then we pray over them. We donate them to the local funeral homes so they can be given to grieving families when they make funeral arrangements."

"That's a beautiful thing, Ava Kate. I like that. Thanks for sharing." Ms. Martha checked her watch. "Anybody else?"

Sam raised her hand before she changed her mind.

"Sam?" Ms. Martha smiled.

"I chose Matthew 22:39: 'Love your neighbor as yourself,' because it made me think of my next door neighbor who's a widow. I chose the resolution so that I'd be more conscientious about thinking of her and being a friend to her."

"That's good, Sam," Ms. Martha said. "How's it going so far?"

"Well, it's really easy. I make it a point to visit her and make sure she isn't as lonely, and she appreciates it. But ..." Sam paused. Sharing this was a little harder than she'd imagined.

"But what?" Ms. Martha asked.

"Well, once I took that Scripture as my resolution, I realized it wasn't just about my actual neighbor, but also neighbors in the whole community. Even some of the kids at school who I don't exactly get along with."

"Oh. So how are you doing with *that* part?"

"I'm not going to say it hasn't been difficult. It has. Sometimes really difficult. But just yesterday, I ran into a girl at the store. We used to be friends, but two years ago, she started acting like she didn't even like me but I've never known what changed, so I felt that I needed to love her by apologizing. So I told her I was sorry for whatever it was I had done to hurt or offend her."

Ms. Martha smiled wide. "How did she respond?"

Sam grinned. "Well, she was a little shocked and seemed like she was going to resist. So I just told her she could either accept my apology or not, but either way, my conscience was clear and I felt good."

"What did she say?" Ms. Martha asked.

Sam grinned wider. "Nothing. I didn't give her a chance. I just told her to have a nice day and I walked off."

The church bells chimed.

Ms. Martha shook her head, but was smiling. "Let's close in prayer, shall we?"

After prayer, Makayla grabbed Sam as she and David headed to the sanctuary. "Were you talking about Aubrey?"

Sam nodded. "I saw her yesterday at Kroger."

"I can't believe you didn't trip over your apology. I would have paid to see her face."

"She put the smirk on, so that's why I had to leave. Figured I shouldn't undo the good start I was going with."

David, clearly bored with their girl-talk, swung his backpack to his other shoulder.

Sam pointed at the USB drive. "Where'd you get that jump drive? I've seen one like it before, but I can't remember where."

David looked at his pack and touched the key-shaped drive. "This one?"

She nodded.

"They're the ones custom designed for our group." He tilted his head toward Makayla. "She should have some."

Maybe that's where she'd seen it before.

"Sam," Dad whispered from behind her.

She turned.

"Mom's got a bit of a headache and needs to lie down. We need to go on home."

"Is she okay?"

"Yes. She says her sinuses feel clogged with the weather changes."

"I'll call you later," Sam told Makayla. She smiled at David. "It was very nice to meet you. I hope you come visit again."

She rushed off with her father toward the car.

CHAPTER NINETEEN

S o that's how it uninstalled." Makayla finished and licked her lips, her nervousness evident on her face.

Mrs. Trees stared at her from across her desk.

Sam pushed her leg against Makayla's in silent support. Makayla's mom sat straight in the chair next to Makayla, looking as uncomfortable as Chewy did when Baby Kitty curled up and went to sleep in the dog's bed.

"The copy is currently being analyzed by the department's cyber unit," Sam's dad said, standing against the wall.

"I'm very impressed," Mr. Alexander replied. "I didn't realize we had such advanced computer science students here at Joe T. Robinson Middle School."

Makayla's mother squared her shoulders. "My daughter is part of a government funded computer

research demographic group. They work on very difficult and complex computer programming issues."

Yeah! Go, Mrs. Ansley. Sam sent silent kudos in her
mind. She winked at Makayla.

"Well. I'm relieved the issue has been resolved." Mrs.
Trees glared at Makayla. "And very relieved that any
further damage wasn't done."

Sam bit her tongue to stop herself from telling the
principal that they should all be extremely grateful to
Makayla. If it hadn't been for her, the system would
still be infected and report cards would still be held
hostage.

But she thought better about saying that. Dad
would probably kill her.

"You girls can go back to class now."

Sam and Makayla stood. Sam kept her gaze down.
No telling what she might be tempted to say if she
looked Mrs. Trees in the eye —

That's why it looked so familiar.

"Mrs. Trees, where did you get this jump drive?" Sam
reached over and grabbed the key shaped drive with
the zebra head sitting on the principal's desk.

"Excuse me, young lady?" Mrs Trees said, holding out
her hand to receive the jump drive back.

"Sam," her dad said, his tone telling her to drop the
question immediately.

But she had to press on.

Sam turned to her best friend. "Mac, you said some

of the people in your group create viruses so y'all can learn how to break them down and delete them, right?"

Makayla nodded.

"Do y'all ever put those on drives? Like that one?"

Makayla's eyes widened. "Yes. Those are the only drives we're allowed to put them on so we don't accidently put them on a PC and infect them." She covered her mouth with her hand. Her eyes went wide.

Sam turned to her father. "Dad."

He held up his hand. "I got it." Dad faced Mrs. Trees. "I need to see that drive, please."

She only hesitated it a moment before she handed it to him. He handed it to Makayla. "Where's the closest computer we can use?"

"EAST lab," Sam replied.

"Let's go," he said, opening the door. Everyone followed.

"Mr. Sanderson, I'm not sure I follow," Mrs. Trees began.

Dad glanced at her over his shoulder. "Let us check this out first, and then I will brief you."

They headed into the EAST lab. Mrs. Shine looked up as they entered. "Hello there."

"Hi, Mrs. Shine. We need to use the MacBook for a second," Sam said.

"Certainly." She waved at the one at the end of the row.

Makayla sat down and gently inserted the drive.

Sam, Mrs. Ansley, Mrs. Trees, Mr. Alexander, and Sam's dad all hovered around her.

"Do you remember enough of the code to recognize it?" Sam's dad asked.

Makayla looked at Sam, excitement burning in her expression.

Sam sighed. "She doesn't have to, Dad. She has a copy. I made it for her." She nodded at Makayla. "Go ahead and compare them."

Makayla pulled Sam's jump drive out of her backpack and stuck it in another USB port.

Dad narrowed his eyes at Sam. "We'll discuss that later."

Great. She was grounded for life.

"It's the same one, Mr. Sanderson," Makayla said as she split screen to look at the files on both of the jump drives. "Exactly the same."

"What's going on?" Mrs. Trees asked. "Officer Bill found that drive on the ground before we broke for Christmas vacation. He gave it to Mrs. Darrington, who gave it to me. I plugged it into my computer to see if there was any student's name on it, but there was only gibberish. Now please tell me why it's so important."

Sam swallowed. This was priceless. "Mrs. Trees, you unknowingly installed the virus on the system."

"What? I did no such thing." She cocked her hip out.

"Only students in my group have those specific drives, Mrs. Trees. And there aren't any other Robinson students in my group. The drive must have fallen out of my backpack when I was running to catch the bus or something," Makayla said. "That's why the virus wasn't set up to cause permanent damage. None of the viruses we create are that destructive." She shook her head. "I didn't even realize my drive was missing. I was busy over break and then with getting back to school and the weather . . ." Makayla's voice wavered, then trailed off.

"Mrs. Trees," Sam's father said, "the virus was created as part of the special group Makayla's in. The drive must have accidently fallen out of her backpack. When you put it in your computer to see if you could identify who it belonged to, it installed the virus."

"But I did that before we left for Christmas break."

Makayla nodded. "The virus was set to go only into a numeric based program. It probably sorted through the programs on your system and the grading system best matched what it needed. When the program was activated, it would shut itself down, then when restarted, the virus would run and infect just that program."

"Very clever," Mr. Alexander said.

"Well," Mrs. Trees said, blinking rapidly. "I had no idea. I never would have put — " she shook her head and frowned at Makayla. "The school board will have to investigate the violations of such an infection — "

"So there was never any intent to tamper with grades. There's been no crime. No one is to blame," Sam's dad interrupted. "And everything has been resolved."

Sam blew out a slow breath. "I guess it's like that old saying, huh: no harm, no foul." She smiled at her best friend, who snuck a smile back.

"For the most part, that's right, pumpkin," Dad said, then leaned over and whispered in Sam's ear, "Except for a certain somebody who deliberately disobeyed me and will be grounded for two weeks."

● ● ●

**... The entire school owes a huge debt of gratitude to Makayla Ansley for removing the virus from our computer system and assisting in solving the mystery. And a most sincere apology to the transfer student who was incorrectly associated with the virus.
~ Sam Sanderson and Aubrey Damas, reporting**

DISCUSSION QUESTIONS

1. Do you make New Year's resolutions? Do you sometimes find them hard to stick to like Sam does? Why?

2. Sam chose to "love her neighbor" (Matthew 22:39), but realized this doesn't mean just her *actual* neighbor, Mrs. Willis. Do you think Sam does a good job of loving her neighbors, family, and friends in the book?

3. When Felicia tells Sam why she was expelled, Sam decides not to write about it. Would you protect a friend's secret, even if that meant missing out on a big opportunity?

4. At one point, Sam worries her stories might hurt innocent people. Have you ever accidently hurt someone when you thought you were doing something good? What happened?

5. Sam apologizes to Aubrey although she has no idea why Aubrey is upset with her. Would you

apologize to someone who was mean to you, even if you hadn't done anything wrong?

6. For a moment, Sam believes that Luke's dad might have gotten angry and hurt him. If you were Sam, what would you do? Would you talk to your friend? Your parents? Someone at school?

7. In the end, it turns out the virus was put on the computer system accidentally. Who did you think was tampering with the grades? Why?

8. When Sam's mom is in the airplane accident, Sam is very scared and prays with Makayla. When you're afraid, does praying make you feel better? How do you pray in times like those?

9. Some of the other kids in Sam's youth group based their New Year's resolutions off the Bible. If you were to choose a Scripture for your resolution, what would it be?

10. We don't learn why Aubrey is upset with Sam, but we do learn she is holding a grudge. What is a grudge? Have you ever been angry with a person for a long time? Did you tell them that you were angry? Why or why not?

11. During the winter storm, Sam rescues a kitten. Have you ever rescued a pet or an animal? What did you do to save them?

12. Sam's mom tells Sam that she should be brave even when she's afraid or things aren't going her way. Do you remember a time when it was really hard to be brave? What happened?

13. At one point, Sam has to look through the comments on her article to "profile" people who may be involved with the grade tampering. What do you think about profiling? What are some good and bad things about it?

14. When Makayla is looking for the virus, she doubts herself and isn't sure she's the right person for the job. But Sam believes in her all along. Have you ever had someone believe in you when you didn't believe in yourself?

15. Luke tells Sam a big secret about his science project—that he didn't do it all on his own. If you were Sam, what would you do? Would you tell Luke to confess? Would you talk to a teacher? Or would you keep Luke's secret like Sam does?

16. Have you ever gotten a bad grade when you knew you'd done better? What did you do about it?

17. When the false report cards come out, a lot of students are worried their parents will be upset or won't believe the grades are wrong. How would your parents or guardians react if that happened to you?

SAMANTHA SANDERSON OFF THE RECORD

18. Sam and Makayla are best friends but have very different interests: Sam loves reporting and cheerleading while Makayla is into computers and karate. Do you have a friend who is different from you? What are the similarities that bring you together?

19. In the end, how do you think Mrs. Trees felt when she learned she was the one who let the virus loose? What would you do if you were her?

20. If you were Felicia and you thought Sam had spilled your secret, how would you react? Would you give your friend the benefit of the doubt?

Samantha Sanderson At The Movies

Robin Caroll

Sam Sanderson is an independent, resourceful, high-tech cheerleader. She dreams of becoming an award-winning journalist like her mother, and so she's always looking for articles she can publish in the middle-school paper (where she secretly hopes to become editor). And with a police officer for a father, Sam is in no short supply for writing material.

It seemed like the perfect reporting opportunity when an explosive device is found in the local theater. Sam gets the lead on this developing and controversial story—controversial because the movie theater has recently come under attack by a renowned, outspoken atheist for allowing a local church to show Christian movies. Sam's police-officer father happens to be heading the investigation, and Sam can't resist doing some sleuthing of her own with the help of her best friend Makayla's techno-genius. But when Sam's theories end up being printed in the school paper, she lands in big trouble—and danger!

Samantha Sanderson On The Scene

Robin Caroll

What if getting to the bottom of a mystery means learning how to love your enemy? As Samantha and the rest of the middle schoolers prepare for the upcoming Spring Fest, "mean girl" Nikki faces the reality that her parents are getting divorced. Samantha has a hard time sympathizing—Nikki has never been very nice to anyone, let alone Samantha. But when Nikki becomes the victim of a string of attacks, Sam takes it upon herself and uses her super sleuth abilities to get to the bottom of the bullying. After all, articles on bullying are just what the school paper needs instead of all that silly fluff like popularity tips. Samantha enlists the help of her tech-savvy BFF, Makayla, but while the two track down clues, they leave a trail of trouble behind—and may even be directly responsible for the break-in of their very own school's computer lab!

Samantha Sanderson is a resourceful seventh grader with the extraordinary dream to become an award-winning journalist. Sam and her best friend, Makayla, are always sniffing out the next big mystery to report in the school paper—that is, when they aren't busy navigating the crazy world of middle school, faith, and friends.

Available in stores and online!

The Good News Shoes
Written by Jill Osborne

**Riley Mae and the
Rock Shocker Trek**

**Riley Mae and the
Ready Eddy Rapids**

**Riley Mae and the
Sole Fire Safari**

Available in stores and online!

NIV Faithgirlz! Bible, Revised Edition

Every girl wants to know she's totally unique and special. These Bibles say that with Faithgirlz! sparkle. Through the many in-text features found only in the *Faithgirlz! Bible*, girls will grow closer to God as they discover the journey of a lifetime.

Features include:

- **Book introductions**—Read about the who, when, where, and what of each book.

- **Dream Girl**—Use your imagination to put yourself in the story.

- **Bring It On!**—Take quizzes to really get to know yourself.

- **Is There a Little (Eve, Ruth, Isaiah) in You?**—See for yourself what you have in common.

- **Words to Live By**—Check out these Bible verses that are great for memorizing.

- **What Happens Next?**—Create a list of events to tell a Bible story in your own words.

- **Oh, I Get It!**—Find answers to Bible questions you've wondered about.

- The complete NIV translation

- Features written by bestselling author Nancy Rue.

Available in stores and online!

Faithgirlz Journal
My Doodles, Dreams and Devotion

Looking for a place to dream, doodle, and record your innermost questions and secrets? You will find what you seek within the pages of the Faithgirlz Journal, which has plenty of space for you to discover who you are, explore who God is shaping you to be, or write down whatever inspires you. Each journal page has awesome quotes and powerful Bible verses to encourage you on your walk with God! So grab a pen, colored pencils, or even a handful of markers. Whatever you write is just between you and God.

Available in stores and online!